TRANSFORMERS EARTHSPARK
THE OFFICIAL GUIDEBOOK

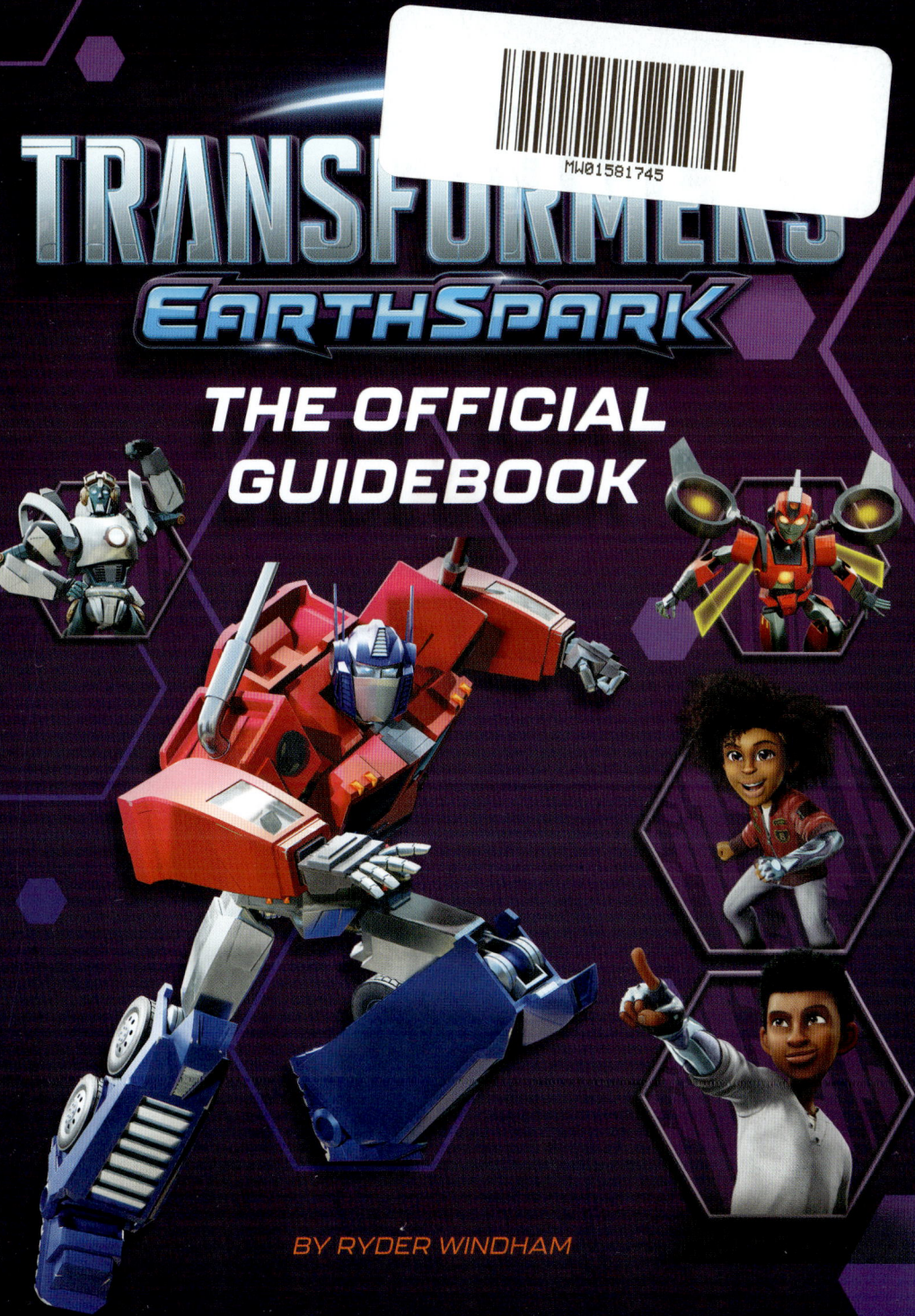

BY RYDER WINDHAM

SIMON SPOTLIGHT
NEW YORK   LONDON   TORONTO   SYDNEY   NEW DELHI

SIMON SPOTLIGHT
An imprint of Simon & Schuster Children's Publishing Division
1230 Avenue of the Americas, New York, New York 10020
This Simon Spotlight paperback edition July 2023
TRANSFORMERS and all related characters are trademarks of Hasbro and are used with permission.
TRANSFORMERS © 2023 Hasbro. All Rights Reserved. Transformers: EarthSpark TV series © 2023 Hasbro/Viacom International Inc. All Rights Reserved. Nickelodeon is a trademark of Viacom International Inc.
All rights reserved, including the right of reproduction in whole or in part in any form.
SIMON SPOTLIGHT and colophon are registered trademarks of Simon & Schuster, Inc.
For information about special discounts for bulk purchases, please contact Simon & Schuster Special Sales at 1-866-506-1949 or business@simonandschuster.com.
Manufactured in China 0223 SCP
2 4 6 8 10 9 7 5 3 1
ISBN 978-1-6659-3303-2 (pbk)
ISBN 978-1-6659-3304-9 (ebook)

Handwriting guide
Mo's handwriting
Robby's handwriting
Alex's handwriting
Dot's handwriting

Meet the Maltos! Jawbreaker, Hashtag, Thrash, Nightshade, Twitch, Dot Malto (Mom), Alex Malto (Dad), me, and Robby

Hi! My name is Morgan Malto, but my friends call me Mo. And if you're reading this guidebook, you must be a GOOD friend because my family and I would never let just anybody read it!

A lot has happened recently. First, my parents and my older brother, Robby, and I moved from a big city to a small farm. Then Robby and I got two new siblings. And not long after that, we got three MORE siblings. So now there's a total of SEVEN kids in my family, and if you think that's fantastic . . .

My new siblings aren't human beings. They're living robots, also known as TRANSFORMERS bots!

But because they're also kids like me and Robby, they're super fun to play with!

Unfortunately, there's one big problem with our situation. We have to keep the Transformers bots in my family a secret! That's because some people don't like robots and think all Transformers bots should be locked up, even though many of them are nice and helpful, and fun too!

Which is why my family and I created this guidebook, because we want YOU to know all about Transformers bots. We're sure you'll want them to be your friends too!

WELCOME TO WITWICKY

Have you ever heard of Witwicky, Pennsylvania? It's a rural suburb of Philadelphia. I didn't know anything about Witwicky before my family and I moved here! Witwicky has a town square and an area that the locals call "downtown," with stores and markets and office buildings. But compared with Philadelphia, the city where we used to live, Witwicky is tiny!

Moving from such a big city to a farm in the country was quite a change for us, especially for me and my brother, Robby. We missed our friends, and we also missed having a good internet connection!

But not long after we arrived, I realized Witwicky has a lot to offer. Like wide open spaces, fresh air, and more trees than you can imagine. I love exploring the Witwicky Woods! Oh, and another major attraction is the Witwicky Racetrack, a great place to watch fast cars in action.

Why did we move to Witwicky? Because my mom took a job as a park ranger for the National Park Service. However, she soon learned that her REAL job is for a secret organization that works with

When you go for a walk in Witwicky Woods, you never know who you might run into!

Transformers robots! More about that later.
   Speaking of Transformers robots, my dad is a history professor, and he's been writing a book about the history of them. So if you're curious about them and how they wound up in Witwicky, you can count on Professor Alex Malto to tell you everything you need to know!

   —Mo Malto

The Witwicky Town Square has lots of shops. I'm looking forward to visiting the bookstore!

A BRIEF HISTORY OF TRANSFORMERS ROBOTS

By Professor Alex Malto

You may have read about the adventures of Transformers robots—also called "bots"—in books and comics, and also seen them in news reports. Maybe you've even played with the toys, most of which have moving parts that allow you to change the robots into their alt modes, alternate shapes such as cars, trucks, airplanes, beasts, dinosaurs, and machinery!

If you want to learn about Cybertronian history, Alex Malto literally wrote the book!

But did you know Transformers robots are LIVING, and that they come from a planet that's older than Earth? Incredibly, some Transformers bots are not only millions of years old, but are also still alive and fully functional!

Their story begins on the distant planet Cybertron, home to many mechanical, technological life-forms. These Cybertronians are sentient beings, with thoughts and feelings that make each one of them a unique individual. In that way, Transformers robots are very much like humans!

And just as humans need food, water, and blood to sustain their lives, Transformers robots require Energon, a blue substance that serves as their fuel. But because their bodies are composed of metal, they are much stronger than humans!

As their name implies, Transformers bots also have a natural ability to alter their shapes and appearances, which helps them to survive and blend in with their surroundings. Each bot starts off with their original body, which they call their "protoform." Inside every protoform is a bio-mechanism called a Transformation Cog, or a T-Cog for short. T-Cogs enable protoforms to scan vehicles or other objects, change from their protoforms to their selected alt mode, and operate integrated weapon systems.

If you're wondering why the robots have built-in weapons, the reason is that the Transformers robots were at war with one another—fighting for Energon and control of Cybertron—for millions of years. Fortunately for us, a good number of bots have chosen to only use their weapons to defend humanity!

An artist's rendering of the ancient planet Cybertron, the original home of Transformers robots.

Autobot leader Optimus Prime faced off against Megatron, leader of the Decepticons, during the Transformers war.

AUTOBOTS & DECEPTICONS

There are two distinct types of Cybertronian Transformers robots: Autobots and Decepticons. Both types have similar robot bodies and shape-changing abilities, but are distinguishable by different insignias—one for Autobots and one for Decepticons—that they wear like badges. The Autobots and Decepticons also have different leaders and traditions.

An Autobot known as the Prime carries the Matrix of Leadership. The Prime leads all the Autobots and always consults with allies before making important decisions. The Autobots work together to promote peace for everyone.

The leader of the Decepticons does not have an official title, but is, quite simply, the most powerful Decepticon.

The Decepticon leader expects his subjects to follow his orders without question.

Millions of years ago, the Autobot leader Optimus Prime and the Decepticon leader Megatron joined together and led a revolution to end inequality on Cybertron. But eventually, their different beliefs and goals put them at odds with each other and ignited the civil war known as the Transformers war. Cybertron became a gigantic battle zone, and when the Autobots and Decepticons traveled to Earth, they brought the Transformers war with them.

Autobot

Decepticon

You can tell if a bot is an Autobot or Decepticon by their insignia!

THE ALLSPARK

The AllSpark is an ancient and powerful artifact, and it gives Transformers robots their "spark" that brings them to life! Without the AllSpark, the planet Cybertron could grow weak and die.

For millions of years, Decepticons and Autobots fought for possession of the AllSpark. The Autobots wanted to preserve the AllSpark and keep their home planet alive. But the Decepticons wanted to use the AllSpark's awesome power as a weapon to raise countless legions of new warriors, and to conquer every world in the universe!

For a brief period, an underground laboratory in San Francisco contained the powerful AllSpark.

SPACEBRIDGES

Spacebridges create portals for instant travel between distant worlds. Ancient Cybertronians used Spacebridges to connect their colonies across the universe as they searched for precious Energon.

To prevent the Decepticons from obtaining the AllSpark on Cybertron, Optimus Prime used a Spacebridge to launch the AllSpark far across the universe. Incredibly, the AllSpark landed

The Spacebridge that once connected Earth and Cybertron

on Earth. Many centuries later, Cybertronians abandoned Cybertron and traveled to Earth. They located the AllSpark, and the terrible fight continued between the Autobots and Decepticons!

Optimus Prime knew the Decepticons would never stop trying to get the AllSpark for their own wicked goals. He also knew Cybertron had grown weak without the AllSpark. So he made a desperate plan to use a Spacebridge to send the AllSpark back to Cybertron and then destroy the Spacebridge.

If his plan succeeded, the Transformers war would be over, and the AllSpark would revive Cybertron! However, with the Spacebridge destroyed, the Autobots and Decepticons would be stranded on Earth and unable to return to their home planet.

But Optimus Prime could not carry out his plan alone. He needed help.

He needed Megatron.

Hoping to end the Transformers war and save the planet Cybertron, Megatron helped Optimus Prime and the Autobots to launch the AllSpark through a Spacebridge.

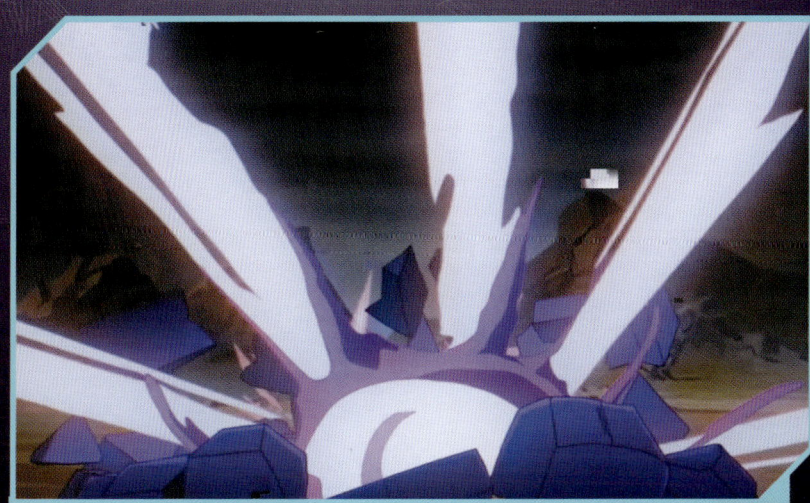

After Megatron hurled the AllSpark through the Spacebridge, Optimus Prime blasted and destroyed the Spacebridge, cutting off access between Earth and Cybertron.

ENEMIES NO MORE!

Because Optimus Prime and Megatron had been at war for millions of years, most Cybertronians and Earthlings had a difficult time imagining the possibility that the two might stop fighting. Yet while Megatron maintained that he would not rest until he conquered all the Autobots, Optimus Prime always kept in mind that long ago, before the Transformers war, he and Megatron had once been friends. Optimus Prime always believed that they could be friends again.

When Megatron met Lieutenant Dorothy Malto on a battlefield, he realized that she cared more about his Decepticon soldiers than he did, and that she was braver than him too. For the first time in his life, Megatron felt ashamed for all the destruction he had caused.

Fifteen years after the end of the Transformers war, Megatron and Optimus Prime reunite with their friend and ally Dot Malto in Witwicky.

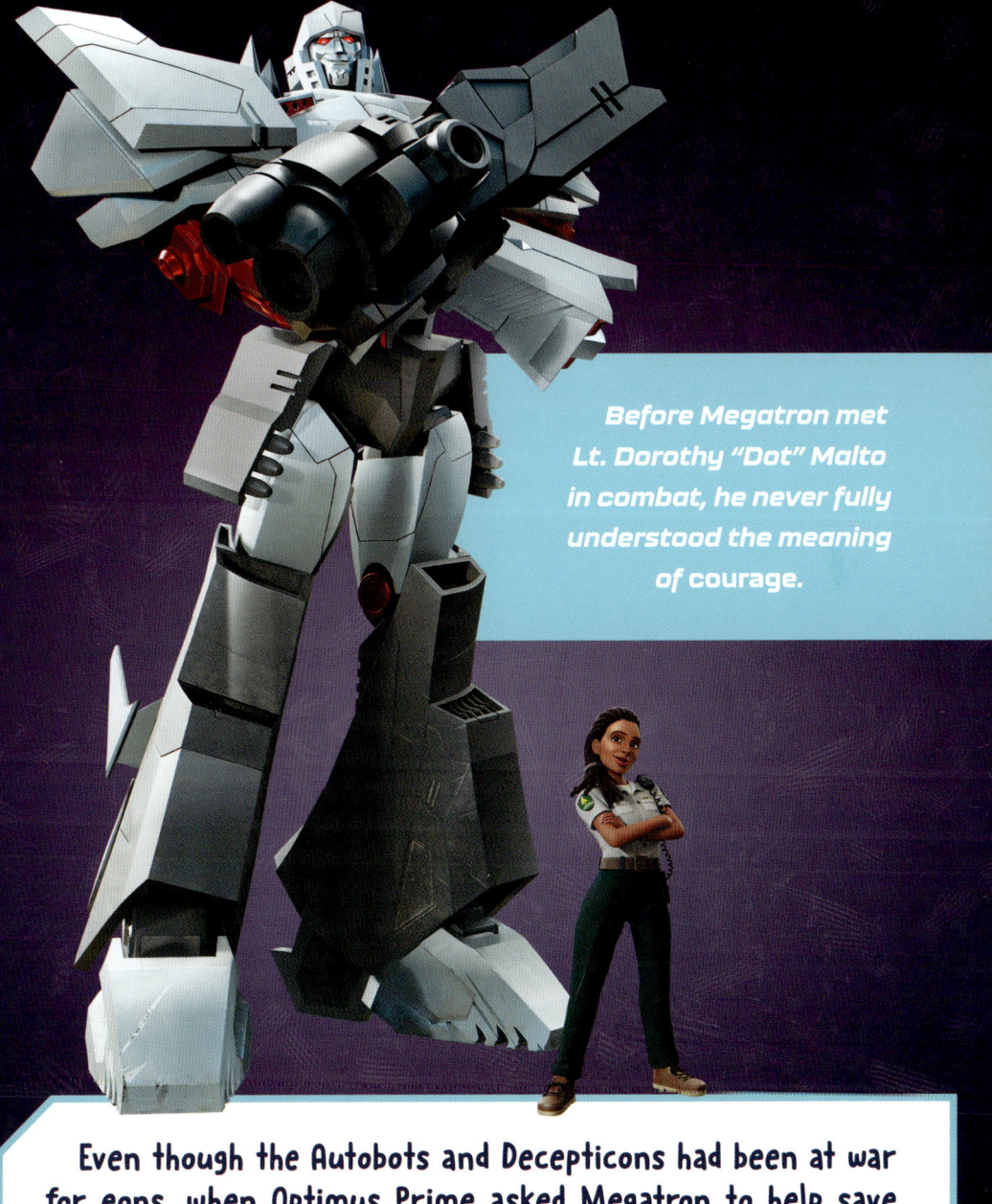

Before Megatron met Lt. Dorothy "Dot" Malto in combat, he never fully understood the meaning of courage.

Even though the Autobots and Decepticons had been at war for eons, when Optimus Prime asked Megatron to help save Cybertron, Megatron listened. And at long last, Megatron was ready to be helpful, and Optimus Prime and Megatron began fighting side by side against the Decepticon forces!

The birdbath was already on our property when we moved here. Dad added the plastic flamingos!

MALTO FAMILY FARM

Before my family moved to Witwicky, I think my father was more excited than anyone about living on a farm with nearby woodlands. That's because Dad grew up in a rural area in the Philippines and has a lot of happy memories of exploring the woods with his grandfather. Also, Dad loves to cook, and now that we're on a farm, he has plenty of land for growing lots of fruits and vegetables for our household meals. And if he grows more than we can use, he plans on donating the surplus produce to a local food bank!

I don't know how old our house is, but I'm pretty sure it's older than our former home in Philadelphia. We also have more rooms! Mom and Dad say we're lucky that the farm's previous owners took good care of the place, so we didn't have to do any expensive repairs or remodeling before we moved in. When Dad first stepped into the kitchen, he said, "You'd better get your umbrellas, because I can't wait to cook up a storm!"

If you smell something cooking in the Malto family kitchen, you can bet Dad is preparing another delicious meal for everyone. His specialties include lumpia (Filipino spring rolls), longganisa (Filipino sausages), and bibingka (Filipino coconut-rice cake)!

My parents share a minivan, and Mom knew that she'd also get a vehicle for her new job with the Park Service, so she was concerned that the property wouldn't have a garage. But then she looked inside the farm's big red barn and realized there was space for several cars. Little did we know that the barn would soon come in handy as a living space for new members of our family!

The barn may look ordinary from the outside, but after some remodeling, the inside is amazing!

DOROTHY "DOT" MALTO

Pardon me if I brag about my beautiful wife, Dottie!

First thing you gotta know about Dot Malto... For her, family ALWAYS comes first. I sincerely believe that her unconditional love for all of us is her superpower!

Dot and I met at university, when we were taking the same class, Color Theory in Literature. The first time we danced together, it was raining, and the name of the song was "Purple Thunder." All these years later, whenever I see the color purple, I think of my relationship with Dot!

She's also a veteran of the Transformers war, and she served as a lieutenant with Optimus Prime and the Autobots. Fifteen years ago, in the final battle of that war, she was doing her best to move injured Cybertronians to safety when she confronted the Autobots' greatest enemy, the Decepticon named Megatron!

Dot and Megatron formed a friendship that's founded on a mutual respect for each other's intelligence, and Dot's belief that anyone can learn from their mistakes and grow.

She didn't run away or try to attack Megatron. She stood her ground and said, "I'm saving your wounded, Megatron. Either help or get out of my way." And only then did Megatron realize that Dot was indeed helping injured Decepticons as well as Autobots. Dot's actions changed Megatron for the better!

Still in the battlefield, Megatron was helping Dot with the wounded when Dot was caught in a blast and lost her right leg below the knee. Megatron himself carried her to Optimus Prime so she could receive proper medical treatment.

Dot now wears a prosthetic leg. She's not bitter about her experience because she accomplished something incredible, something no one else had ever done: she gained the trust and friendship of Megatron.

We're all so proud of her!

—Alex Malto

Here's Dot all suited up for ranger duty!

ALEX MALTO

Nobody rattles off dad jokes like my father, Alex Malto. I am not exaggerating. He is constantly cracking jokes, and it seems like he has one for any and every occasion!

Recently, at the dinner table, Dad noticed Robby was sitting very still, so he said, "What did the petrified boy say about my cooking? 'It rocks!'"

Pretty awful, right? And he's got a million of them!

One thing he's serious about is his work. He has a PhD in history, and he's writing a series of books about the history of Transformers robots. When it comes to checking information and confirming facts about Cybertronians, Dad doesn't joke around.

He's also incapable of hiding his admiration for the Autobots. He's a total fanboy! His favorite

Because Dad is such a big fan of Bumblebee, imagine how surprised he was when he finally got to meet his hero. Bumblebee even proclaimed Dad an honorary Autobot!

Dad probably has more Bumblebee collectibles than anyone else, and he asked Bumblebee to autograph each item!

Autobot has always been Bumblebee, and he has a huge collection of Bumblebee stuff.

When the Transformers war ended, Bumblebee pretty much disappeared for fifteen years, but Dad refused to believe Bumblebee was gone forever. He was always optimistic that Bumblebee was alive and would return someday. "Be an Optimist Prime," Dad said, "not a Negatron!"

When Dad actually met Bumblebee, it was a rare occasion that he didn't tell a joke with a bad pun. Because he was speechless! Oh, and another thing . . . Dad grew up in Bohol, in the Philippines, and is very proud of his heritage. So he was delighted to learn that Bumblebee has visited Bohol and won drag races at the old Tagbilaran Airport!

Where we live in Witwicky, the internet service is so bad that Robby and I tried getting a signal from the top of our barn's roof!

ROBBY MALTO

My brother, Robby, is thirteen years old. I told him this guidebook would include sections about each member of our family, and I asked if he wanted to write about himself. He said, "I'm too busy with other stuff."

Too busy, huh? You had your chance, Robby! Now I get to say whatever I want about you. Ha!

Robby Malto enjoys being the center of attention. And he often "forgets" his chores because he always has something "more important" to do.

Okay, I'm all through with teasing my brother. Really, that's the only negative stuff I can say about him!

And I really should add . . . Even though he DOES enjoy being the center of attention, he's also a good person, a loyal friend, and a terrific brother! Oh, and he can't stand it when he sees someone who looks like they're feeling left out. For example, one time back in Philadelphia, Robby was playing basketball with a group of friends, and I asked if I could play too. One of the guys said, "No way! We've already got all the players we need for this game."

Robby said, "Mo can fill in for me while I take a breather. If anyone has a problem with that, I guess you'll need to find some new players."

That's EXACTLY what he said. Because it's important to Robby that everyone should feel included. How cool is that?!

When Robby starts playing one of his video games, he sometimes loses track of the rest of the world!

In the Malto household, dinner is always our special family time!

MO MALTO

I guess I have to tell you about myself now. Where to begin? Yikes!

Oh, I just remembered . . . A few months ago, when I was still going to school in Philadelphia, my homeroom teacher asked all the students to write a short essay about ourselves, and our hopes and goals for the summer. Here's what I wrote!

MY SUMMER PLANS, by Mo Malto (age 9)

My family and I are moving to a farm in Witwicky where I don't know anyone. I have friends here in Philadelphia, and it makes me sad to think that I won't be able to see them anymore. But I'm also sort of excited to move, and to live on a farm. I haven't actually seen our new home in real life yet. I've only seen pictures online, but it looks really nice.

The farm has apple trees and large fields where cows can graze. My dad says we'll be drinking fresh milk with our homemade apple pies. Yum!

What if we don't make any friends until school starts in September? I love my brother, and Robby and I get along okay, but we might get on each other's nerves if we're together all day every day this summer!

My mom and dad believe life is an adventure, so my goal is to have the most adventurous summer ever. Maybe I'll even make friends who love wrestling as much as I do!

Our summer adventure kicked in the night that Robby rode off on his bike, and I went after him. What happened next? Read on, my friend!

THE MYSTERIOUS CAVERN

Not long after my family moved to Witwicky, Robby decided that he missed Philadelphia so much that he took off on his bicycle, heading for the city. I followed him on my bike to try to stop him, but then we saw a bunch of spiderlike robots attack a convoy of trucks and vans on the road just ahead of us. We had no idea what was going on, but when one of the robots destroyed a truck, we knew we had to get away, and fast!

We jumped over a safety rail and tumbled down a steep hill. Neither of us got hurt, but both of us were scared by the robots we'd seen on the road. I was also angry with Robby for leaving home without me at night, and he was angry with me for trying to stop him. So he shouted real loud, and then I shouted too!

Robby and I had no idea that spider robots were on the loose in Witwicky until we ran into them! We later learned they're called Arachnamechs.

When Robby and I saw a strange light glowing inside the cave, how could we not want to investigate?

We were still shouting when we saw a weird, golden-green light start to glow nearby. The light came from inside the mouth of a cave! Thinking back, it seemed like our shouts—or maybe our emotions—caused the light to glow.

We entered the cavern and discovered the source of the light: a large gem resting on a natural pedestal next to a pool of cave water. Robby touched the gem and accidentally knocked it over. I was helping him put it back on the pedestal when it suddenly released something that felt like a wave of energy. And then we heard a deep voice say, "Legacy of hope . . ."

Later, we learned that the gem was an ancient Cybertronian artifact called the Emberstone!

THE EMBERSTONE

By Professor Alex Malto

According to Cybertronian history, Quintus Prime was one of the original thirteen Primes who helped create Cybertronian culture. Quintus Prime used an artifact, the Emberstone, to create life on worlds across the universe.

No one knows how or when the Emberstone came to rest within a cavern in Witwicky. But Cybertronians regard the Emberstone as a gift of Quintus Prime, and it seems the purpose of this gift was to create new living robots on Earth!

When they touched the Emberstone, Robby and Mo sensed that there was something unusual about it. Soon, they learned it possessed strange powers, and that it came from another world!

Unfortunately, we later lost the Emberstone during a fight with Decepticons. On the plus side, I can thank Quintus Prime and the Emberstone for bringing five more children into my family!

How long had the Emberstone been in the cave before Robby and Mo discovered it? And did Quintus Prime himself place it there? Sometimes history can be quite a mystery!

Did Robby and I holler when the glowing stone released a weird substance that stretched over our arms? You bet we did! It didn't hurt, but still . . . we were scared!

MEET THE TERRANS

Robby and I were horrified as we watched the Emberstone sprout a glowing, goopy substance that suddenly wrapped around our forearms! The substance looked like it had circuits or some kind of cyber-organic technology inside of it. We shouted as the substance formed into long, fingerless gloves, with sleeves that tightened across our skin. With our free hands, we tugged at the sleeves but couldn't remove them!

We were still struggling with the sleeves when we noticed two figures rising from the nearby pool. The figures were Transformers bots! At first, their eyes were dark, but then the Emberstone went dark, and a moment later the robots' eyes glowed blue. And then they looked straight at me and Robby!

The robots moved, and Robby and I were even more terrified. But instead of moving toward us, the robots had darted behind some rocks on the cavern floor. At the same moment, Robby and I realized that the strange sleeves on our arms were glowing. Right away, we both knew that the robots were just as scared of us as we were of them. Not only that, but we also knew the robots' names!

Twitch and Thrash.

And then they spoke to us. They knew OUR names!

Robby and I were connected to the robots. We didn't understand exactly how we were connected, but we were sure the sleeves had something to do with it. Somehow, the sleeves allowed all of us to share our thoughts and feelings.

And then we weren't afraid of one another anymore, because we all knew and felt the same thing: we were friends!

Robby and I were still wondering about our new sleeves when we saw two figures rising from a pool in the cave. The figures were Twitch and Thrash in their original protoforms!

CYBER-SLEEVES

By Professor Alex Malto

I thought I knew a lot about Cybertronian history and technology, but I must admit that until I saw the things wrapped around Robby's right arm and Mo's left arm, I wasn't familiar with Cyber-Sleeves. I'd also never heard of new Transformers robots rising from a sludgy pool in a glowing cave!

But thanks to some helpful Autobot friends, I now have a better understanding of Cyber-Sleeves, which are also known as bio-Energon sleeves. They're made from ancient Cybertronian technology and enable organic life-forms to emotionally link with living robots. When Robby and Mo touched the Emberstone that they found in a cave, the Emberstone gave them Cyber-Sleeves at the same moment that it gave life to Twitch and Thrash, the first Transformers robots born on Earth!

Thanks to the powers of the Cyber-Sleeves, Robby and Mo feel strong emotional connections with Twitch and Thrash. The connections work both ways, and all around!

When Mo and Robby go to school, they have to be careful not to let their classmates and teachers see their Cyber-Sleeves, especially on highly emotional days!

Because of the Cyber-Sleeves, Robby, Mo, and their new siblings have a powerful bond that allows each of them to feel when the others are happy, sad, or scared. When the siblings share emotions, the Cyber-Sleeves light up! Watching the colors of the Cyber-Sleeves, it's clear that Robby is especially in tune with Twitch while Mo is very much in tune with Thrash.

And so you know, when I say "the siblings," I do mean SIBLINGS! Twitch and Thrash are definitely part of the Malto family now, as are three more Terrans who came into our lives later. I feel so lucky to be their dad!

Because Cyber-Sleeves are a permanent physical link and can't be removed, Robby and Mo conceal their Cyber-Sleeves under their clothes. I wonder if Cyber-Sleeves ever make their skin feel itchy. I must ask them!

TWITCH

After Robby and I met Twitch and Thrash in the cavern, we were bringing them to our home when I told Robby that I could hardly wait to tell Dad that we'd adopted two Transformers robots. But Robby said we couldn't tell Dad or Mom because Twitch and Thrash were totally new Transformers robots. He thought because they were born on Earth, someone would take them away for sure! So we explained to Twitch and Thrash that they should hide in our barn, and that we'd try to figure out how to tell our parents about them so they could stay with us forever.

But the next morning, Robby and I still hadn't talked with our parents when we saw Twitch and Thrash outside our house, where our parents might see them! Hoping to get them out of view, I asked if they wanted to play hide-and-seek. Twitch said, "A competition? I'm listening!" And then she and Thrash darted off to hide in the yard. Right then, I could tell that Twitch lives for competition!

And she can make anything-even household chores-into a game. Oh, another example . . . Robby and Twitch were playing in the woods, and Twitch bet Robby that she could name more birds than he could. But instead of identifying birds by their traditional or scientific names, she invented a bunch of silly names for random birds, like Leslie, Mike, Kerri with an "i," Kerry with a "y," and Spizwig. Pretty funny, huh?

Twitch's high-octane brain is always working as she analyzes situations and sorts out possible plans of action! And with her take-charge personality, Twitch is also a natural leader. She meshes well with Robby!

Twitch loves to play games, and if she doesn't know the rules to a game, she'll make up rules on the spot!

In the woods, Twitch and Robby had a contest to see who could hit more targets. Robby demonstrated that he's good at throwing rocks at boulders, but Twitch used her laser to blast a hole straight through a boulder!

Twitch was birdwatching for the first time in Witwicky Woods when she accidentally scanned one of Wheeljack's drones.

TWITCH'S ALT MODE

Robby was with Twitch the first time she changed into her vehicle mode, so Robby is writing this part!

My dad is an expert on Transformers robots, and he's told me lots of stories and information about them. According to him, most bots spend some time looking at cars and other types of vehicles before they select an alternative mode to disguise themselves. That's because bots can't change their alt modes the way people change clothes. I don't remember all the details from Dad's explanation about Cybertronian technology, but essentially, after a bot converts into their alt mode, they have to live with their choice!

Minutes after Twitch transformed into her alt mode, she took Robby flying!

So how much time did it take for Twitch to select her alt mode? Practically no time at all! In fact, even she admitted that her "choice" happened by accident.

It happened the day after Mo and I met Twitch and Thrash. We were all playing in the woods when Twitch noticed birds in the trees. She climbed up a tree to get a better view of the birds, but then she spotted a strange drone. Later, we learned the drone belonged to the Autobot named Wheeljack, but at the time I didn't know what it was . . . and Twitch thought it was some kind of bird!

Twitch was just staring at the drone when beams of blue light shot out from her eyes and scanned the drone. She was so surprised that she fell out of the tree! But before she reached the ground, she changed shape in midair. She changed into a drone . . . a drone capable of carrying a passenger: ME!

—Robby Malto

Twitch's propeller blades can create mini-tornadoes to blow away enemies!

THRASH

The morning after Robby and I brought Twitch and Thrash home, we were all playing in the woods when Thrash started juggling two boulders, and then picked me up and added me to the airborne mix. I felt like a circus acrobat! I don't know how much the boulders weighed, but they were obviously heavy, so I was surprised by Thrash's strength, not to mention his juggling skills!

Later that day, Thrash and I were in an alley off Witwicky Town Square, and we ran into an Arachnamech. The Arachnamech pounced on Thrash, but seconds later, Thrash grabbed the Arachnamech, along with several nearby trash-can lids, and he began yet another juggling routine. Then Thrash whipped the Arachnamech straight against the alley's dead

For Thrash's very first dance lesson, I taught him the victory dance!

If you want an idea of Thrash's strength, just look at him juggling boulders as if they were beanbags!

end. For that bit of action, I felt compelled to teach Thrash the art of the victory dance!

Mom and Dad say Thrash has a wild streak, and he's always challenging rules and pushing boundaries. Because he tends to act before thinking, he often gets into trouble! But despite being reckless and unpredictable, Thrash is also as loyal as he is brave. Whenever some danger threatens his family, he races without hesitation to protect them . . . I mean, US!

If Thrash were entirely on his own and didn't have any family ties, I suppose he'd do whatever he wants, whenever he wants. What can I say? He's a rebel! However, judging by the feelings I get from my Cyber-Sleeve, I think I'm the only one who can get Thrash to listen, especially when I say no to any of his plans for some off-the-wall adventure or another. But his plans are always so fun, and it's sometimes hard for me to discourage him!

The moment Thrash saw a motorcycle with a sidecar, he knew he'd found his alt mode!

THRASH'S ALT MODE

Right after Twitch chose a drone for her alternative mode, Thrash was eager to choose his own alt mode too. We were still in the woods at the time, and Thrash briefly considered a squirrel for his alt mode! So I suggested we sneak over to downtown Witwicky, because I knew he'd have way more stuff to pick from there. I invited Robby and Twitch to come along, but they decided to go off and test Twitch's flying capability.

While Thrash and I were looking at parked cars, I told him that I missed my bicycle, which I named Rocinante. Shortly before Robby and I met Thrash and Twitch, we had to ditch our bikes on a bridge to avoid a bunch of spider robots when they attacked a convoy of trucks! Anyway, one of my favorite books is the novel Don Quixote, written by Miguel de Cervantes, and Rocinante is the name of Don Quixote's horse. MY Rocinante was the fastest bike on my block, and had sleek lines and all-terrain tread. I told Thrash that when I rode Rocinante, I felt like a warrior goddess.

I never imagined that talking about my bike might have some influence on Thrash's choice for an alt mode. But later that day, Thrash saw a motorcycle with a sidecar in a garage. He told me that when he saw it, he said out loud, "Rocinante!" He scanned the motorcycle and sidecar and the rest is history.

I think Thrash's choice for his alt mode embodies his attitude. He's spontaneous and daring, but he's also very loyal. His sidecar guarantees he'll never leave me behind!

Thanks to Thrash's sidecar, I can travel with him!

When Megatron joined the Autobots to end the Transformers war, he saw that Optimus Prime always does what he believes is right, no matter the personal cost.

OPTIMUS PRIME

By Professor Alex Malto

Born on the planet Cybertron, Optimus Prime is the leader of the Autobots, and a legend among Transformers robots. For millions of years, he battled power-craving Decepticons as they waged wars, threatened defenseless bots, and depleted Cybertron and other worlds of Energon resources. Despite his reputation as a great warrior, Optimus Prime's goal was never to conquer the Decepticons, but to bring peace and liberty to all Cybertronians. More than anything, Optimus Prime believes freedom is the right of all sentient beings.

Optimus Prime's trusted allies include Elita-1, Bumblebee, and Wheeljack. The Autobot soldiers respect Optimus Prime not just for his courage and resourcefulness but his empathy and patience. While other members of his group may want to respond quickly to dangerous or complicated situations, Optimus Prime remains calm as he considers the best way

Optimus Prime and his allies did not immediately comprehend that Twitch and Thrash were Earth-born Transformers robots, but they soon realized the importance of the young Terrans.

for all to move forward. And when others may be close to losing hope, Optimus Prime always has the strength to inspire them to be hopeful.

Following the Transformers war, Optimus Prime joined forces with Megatron, and agreed to work with the Global Hazard and Ordinance Strike Team (G.H.O.S.T.), a multinational secret agency that functions to track and capture Decepticons. Optimus Prime does not regard G.H.O.S.T. as a perfect ally, but he believes they'll eventually help ALL Transformers robots make a home on Earth.

Upon meeting Twitch and Thrash, Optimus Prime thought they would be well protected if he sent them to G.H.O.S.T.'s headquarters. But soon after, when Optimus Prime had to rescue the Terrans from a renegade scientist, he agreed with Dot Malto that the best place for Twitch and Thrash was with their human siblings, Robby and Mo, in the Malto home!

OPTIMUS PRIME'S ALT MODE

Many Cybertronians can choose to resemble a wide variety of cars that easily blend in with traffic and other environments on Earth, but Optimus Prime's great height and broad girth limited his choices for an alternative mode. Although his shape-shifting body was large enough to accommodate a heavy-duty construction vehicle as a disguise, such vehicles are not known for their ability to achieve high speeds on an open road and would not allow Optimus Prime to race from one battle zone to another without attracting attention.

On a mission in Witwicky, Optimus Prime removes Cybertranian surveillance drones from his trailer.

Which is why Optimus Prime scanned a semitruck, a tractor trailer that appears as commonly on a mountain back road or desert freeway as it does on a city street. Even in a parking lot or rest area, his alt mode allows him to exist virtually unnoticed by humans.

Optimus Prime can detach his trailer, which allows him to load or remove cargo from its inner area. He also uses the trailer to transport his allies through hazardous areas and to deliver captive Decepticons to detention centers.

In his alt mode, Optimus Prime looks like an ordinary semitruck. But as with all Transformers robots, there's more to this "truck" than meets the eye!

MEGATRON

For millions of years, Megatron and his fellow Decepticons battled the Autobots, fighting for Energon and for possession of the AllSpark. Megatron's goal was to unite all Transformers robots, have them travel across the universe, and rule over all other life-forms.

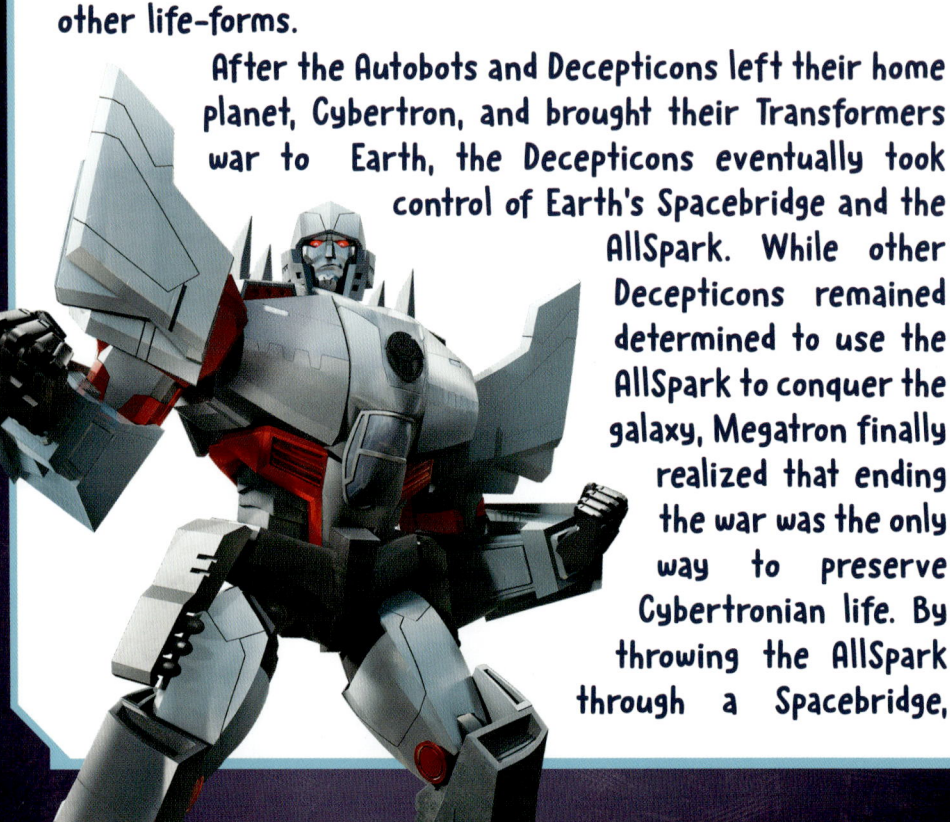

After the Autobots and Decepticons left their home planet, Cybertron, and brought their Transformers war to Earth, the Decepticons eventually took control of Earth's Spacebridge and the AllSpark. While other Decepticons remained determined to use the AllSpark to conquer the galaxy, Megatron finally realized that ending the war was the only way to preserve Cybertronian life. By throwing the AllSpark through a Spacebridge,

Megatron attempted to save Cybertron and also proved his dedication to helping the Autobots protect Earth. When his attempts to peacefully reason with the Decepticons failed, he defected and joined the Autobots. Because of his actions, the Decepticons branded Megatron a traitor.

The Decepticons became even more outraged when Megatron joined Optimus Prime in alliance with G.H.O.S.T., a multinational agency committed to capturing and "detaining" Decepticons. Although Megatron has misgivings about how G.H.O.S.T. operates, he is committed to defending humanity against Decepticon attacks.

Megatron makes every effort to right the wrongs of his past, and to show humans as well as Transformers robots that he has improved himself. Even though some Autobots are reluctant to trust him, Megatron is truly reformed!

Megatron believes the Earth-born Terrans represent the future for Transformers robots.

MEGATRON'S ALT MODE

Just before the end of the Transformers war, when Megatron stopped fighting Optimus Prime and allied with the Autobots, Optimus Prime wanted Megatron to prove his commitment to the Autobots by scanning an Earth vehicle for his new alt mode. Because such action would mean giving up his Cybertronian alt mode, Megatron thought Optimus Prime's command was unfair, and he refused.

However, when Megatron saw a flying Decepticon, the triple-changing giant Astrotrain, attack Lt. Malto's squadron, Megatron realized he needed to take the fight to the skies! Looking to a nearby air base, he saw the last remaining warplane, a tilt-rotor military aircraft capable of vertical takeoffs and landings. Megatron scanned the aircraft, rapidly changed and reconfigured himself, and flew into action against Astrotrain.

Megatron's new alt mode not only helped him defend his new friends, but also prove his loyalty to Optimus Prime!

In his alt mode as a military aircraft, Megatron is capable of traveling swiftly to help his Autobot allies.

BUMBLEBEE

The Autobot named Bumblebee is younger than Optimus Prime, but they have been friends and allies for millions of years! During the Transformers war, when many humans wished Transformers robots had never set foot on Earth, Bumblebee's countless acts of courage seemed to secure his reputation as a hero to humans and Transformers robots alike.

But when the Transformers war ended, and the secret agency G.H.O.S.T. announced it was keeping track of all surviving Autobots and Decepticons, no one could find any sign of Bumblebee! G.H.O.S.T. agents began to wonder if he had escaped from Earth by using some unknown Cybertronian technology. Some agents even wondered if he had joined the

Unlike Optimus Prime and Megatron, Bumblebee does not work with G.H.O.S.T., and he still bears his original Autobot insignia.

Bumblebee carries a Cybertronian first aid kit that contains a medical scanner and Energon patches, which prove useful when a worn-down Thrash requires an energy boost.

Decepticons! As the years went by without any reported sightings of Bumblebee, most humans assumed he was gone forever.

But the truth is . . . Bumblebee is right here in Witwicky!

After the Transformers war, Bumblebee went into hiding for fifteen years. During that time, he carried out secret missions with Optimus Prime and the Autobots. He also managed to have fun by occasionally attempting to break his own speed records! Being careful to avoid detection, Bumblebee snuck into international auto races so he could compete against human drivers and their high-performance cars.

Shortly after Optimus Prime met the Terrans, he called Bumblebee out of hiding and gave him the task of training the Terrans and educating them about the history of Cybertron. At first, Bumblebee balked, but he quickly realized that the Earth-born Transformers bots desperately need Cybertronian guidance. He also realized he has a lot to learn about teaching kids!

BUMBLEBEE'S ALT MODE

Not long after Bumblebee arrived on Earth, he scanned a small yellow car with chrome bumpers and a rear-mounted engine. Small cars were so popular that Bumblebee was generally able to move about without attracting attention.

But there was one problem with the car that Bumblebee had scanned: the stock model did not have a very fast maximum cruising speed. Knowing that he could better help his allies if he could move faster from one hot spot to another, and also hoping to continue avoiding unwanted attention, Bumblebee changed his alt mode to a yellow sports car with black racing stripes.

Because Bumblebee enjoys testing himself at high speed, he sometimes sneaks into competitions at racetracks. But after he disappeared from the public eye, a few G.H.O.S.T. agents noticed yellow cars were winning races all over the world. As much as Bumblebee loves to race, he has to be more careful to prevent G.H.O.S.T. from identifying him!

In his alt mode, Bumblebee passes for a custom-painted, turbo-injected X-12 Limited Edition race car.

ELITA-1

Elita-1 is second-in-command of the Autobots, and has leadership qualities that rival her longtime teammate, Optimus Prime. Like Optimus Prime, she is a very good listener! When meeting with her allies, she listens carefully to everyone and makes sure that all voices are heard before she makes decisions. She quickly solves almost any problem and excels at coming up with clever plans to catch Decepticons! Her allies trust she can always show them how to get things done.

After Elita-1 arrived on Earth, she knew she required an alternate mode that would allow her to move about freely among humans. Despite her talent for solving problems swiftly, she took more time than most bots in choosing her alt mode. She considered countless vehicles over many days, but nothing she saw ever felt right . . . until she saw a red all-terrain 4x4, and her spark told her that was right!

When Elita-1 meets with Dot Malto, Optimus Prime, and Megatron in Witwicky, Megatron notes that Platoon Cyberstrike has reunited!

The wheels that are part of Elita-1's alt mode also serve her well when she's in her bot mode, when she uses her wheels as in-line skates. She can run circles around her enemies before she knocks them off their feet!

Like most Autobots, Elita-1 was Megatron's enemy during the Transformers war. But after Megatron renounced the Decepticons, Megatron and Elita-1 became members of Platoon Cyberstrike, an elite team that also included Optimus Prime and Lt. Dot Malto.

A brave and acrobatic fighter, Elita-1 keeps fit by running and exercising across the naval yard alongside the Delaware River. She uses shipping containers, shifting heaps of scrap metal, and tall piles of rubber tires in the naval yard as her own personal obstacle course. When Bumblebee is not available to teach and train the young Terrans, Elita-1 is always happy to fill in for him.

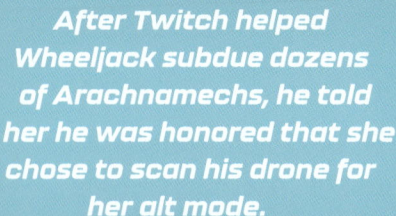

After Twitch helped Wheeljack subdue dozens of Arachnamechs, he told her he was honored that she chose to scan his drone for her alt mode.

WHEELJACK

One of Optimus Prime's Autobot allies, Wheeljack is also a scientist, mechanic, and fearless inventor. He has created many gadgets and weapons to fight and capture Decepticons. His inventions don't always work the way he imagined, but because he learns from his mistakes, even his technological failures are educational.

Wheeljack's successful inventions include a small fleet of semi-autonomous drones. The armor-plated drones are capable of flight and utilize Cybertronian stealth technology to avoid detection. Sophisticated visual and audio sensors enable them to track Decepticons and other targets, and their power supplies and navigational systems allow them to travel through almost any atmosphere and altitude. Used by Wheeljack as well as other members of his team, the drones are also useful for reconnaissance and rescue missions.

In and around the town of Witwicky, Wheeljack soon became aware of damage caused by Arachnamechs. Wheeljack and his drones spent weeks hunting Arachnamechs so he could collect and analyze specimens and hopefully determine their origin. Wheeljack eventually learned that the Arachnamechs are inventions of the former G.H.O.S.T. scientist Dr. Meridian.

Soon after Optimus Prime informed Wheeljack about the existence of two Earth-born Transformers robots, Wheeljack spotted Twitch in her drone mode and mistook her for one of his drones. Because Wheeljack built the drone that Twitch scanned for her alternate mode, Twitch regards Wheeljack as her second father figure, and she calls him Dad2!

Wheeljack's alt mode is a high-performance rally car.

Wheeljack frequently tunes and modifies his parts to make sure his alt mode is always road-ready!

TELETRAAN-1

A Cybertronian computer, Teletraan-1 was the onboard computer of the *Ark*, a massive Autobot starship. The main function of Teletraan-1 was to help the Autobots search for the AllSpark, which Optimus Prime had launched across the universe to prevent the Decepticons from obtaining it. The computer could also scan worlds and asteroids for Energon deposits to refuel the Autobots.

Eventually, the *Ark* arrived on the planet Earth, where the Autobots found not only Energon deposits but also the AllSpark. By the twentieth century, the Autobots were using Teletraan-1's communications systems to monitor television and radio broadcasts as well as satellite transmissions for news about possible threats, natural disasters, and Decepticon activity. By collecting and analyzing such a wide range of data, Teletraan-1 helped the Autobots determine when and where they should go into action, and choose the best options to head off Decepticon attacks.

In the final battle of the Transformers war in San Francisco, Optimus Prime and Megatron—both hoping to end the war and save Cybertron—tried using a Spacebridge to return the AllSpark to Cybertron. G.H.O.S.T. agents subsequently moved Teletraan-1 to their secret headquarters in Witwicky, Pennsylvania. Years later, Optimus Prime and Megatron enlisted the captive Decepticon Soundwave to use Teletraan-1 to find out if the AllSpark arrived on Cybertron. According to Soundwave, Teletraan-1 could not contact or locate Cybertron, leaving Megatron to believe that the AllSpark did not complete its journey home.

After millions of years and journeying far across the universe, the Cybertronian supercomputer Teletraan-1 has come to reside in G.H.O.S.T.'s underground headquarters.

At Witwicky Airfield, Optimus Prime, Megatron, and G.H.O.S.T. cadets observe the thirtieth anniversary of the Human Autobot Alliance.

G.H.O.S.T.

By Dot Malto

When I moved to Witwicky, I thought I was going to be a park ranger, but it turns out G.H.O.S.T. wanted me to work with them. A top-secret military agency, the Global Hazard and Ordinance Strike Team (G.H.O.S.T.) serves to ensure safe Cybertronian-Earth relations. G.H.O.S.T. is so secret that no one seems to know exactly when the agency got started, or how long it has been working with the Autobots to prevent Decepticons from causing trouble.

G.H.O.S.T. agents and soldiers work with Optimus Prime and his team to locate and capture rogue Decepticons. Optimus Prime's principal contact at G.H.O.S.T. is Special Agent Jon Schloder, who serves under the authority of G.H.O.S.T. Executive Agent Karen Croft. Despite the Human Autobot Alliance, Agent Schloder doesn't trust Autobots who have failed to register their whereabouts with G.H.O.S.T., and believes various "missing" Autobots may have joined the Decepticons. Because G.H.O.S.T. has

After Optimus Prime, Megatron, and other Transformers robots became allies of G.H.O.S.T., they replaced their Autobot and Decepticon insignias with special G.H.O.S.T. insignias.

not been able to find any evidence of the famed Autobot named Bumblebee since the end of the Transformers war, Agent Schloder has become obsessed with finding him.

Although the apparent function of G.H.O.S.T. is to protect humans from dangerous robots, some Cybertronians suspect the agency is primarily concerned with its own best interests. In fact, most G.H.O.S.T. agents seem to fear what they don't understand, and also seem to worry that ALL Transformers robots—including Autobots—may be dangerous.

High-ranking G.H.O.S.T. officers include Special Agent Schloder and Executive Agent Croft.

The Ranger Station appears to be a typical building, but it actually conceals G.H.O.S.T. headquarters, a vast underground complex that is accessible by a secret elevator.

G.H.O.S.T. HEADQUARTERS

At the national park in Witwicky, the Ranger Station appears to be an ordinary building. Inside the lobby, ordinary citizens will find small exhibits and posters with information about local wildlife. Beyond the lobby, the station's rooms include small offices and a spacious conference room that provides a meeting space for park rangers.

But individuals with proper security clearance know that the Ranger Station really conceals the underground headquarters for G.H.O.S.T. A hidden elevator in the Ranger Station's conference room transports G.H.O.S.T. agents to the subterranean levels, most of which have chambers sized to accommodate the passage of large Cybertronians. Inside the G.H.O.S.T. Orientation Room, new recruits can read educational pamphlets and brochures about G.H.O.S.T. operations and watch videos that document G.H.O.S.T.'s role in the Human Autobot Alliance.

On an upper level of G.H.O.S.T. headquarters, Optimus Prime and Dot meet to discuss G.H.O.S.T. operations in the Orientation Room.

Another level contains living quarters designed for Optimus Prime, Megatron, and members of their G.H.O.S.T.-approved team. The Transformers robots also have their own "Wreck Room," which features modular structural components, hologram projectors, and automated defense systems that can be reconfigured into countless obstacle courses. The Wreck Room is the perfect place for Autobots and Megatron to test their strength and agility in simulated combat scenarios.

Additional levels contain G.H.O.S.T. communications centers, research laboratories, training rooms, quarters for G.H.O.S.T. agents, and garages and hangars for G.H.O.S.T. vehicles. The most heavily reinforced areas are the lower levels, where G.H.O.S.T. guards oversee a network of cell blocks that house Decepticon captives.

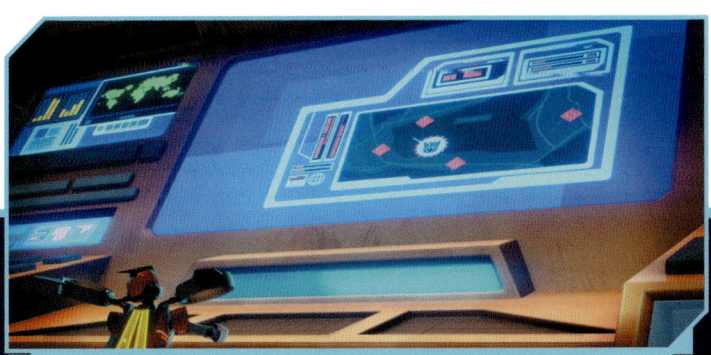

A lower level in G.H.O.S.T. headquarters contains the Wreck Room, a recreational area and mission-training room for G.H.O.S.T.'s Cybertronian allies.

G.H.O.S.T. VEHICLES

G.H.O.S.T. has a covert fleet of military vehicles for hunting down and capturing Decepticons. G.H.O.S.T. agents typically use armored sport utility vehicles (SUVs) and vans to race into danger zones, and transport trucks to move captured Decepticons to G.H.O.S.T. holding facilities and the underground detention center. Dedicated crews of technicians and mechanics make sure the vehicles are ready for action at a moment's notice.

Many G.H.O.S.T. SUVs, vans, and trucks are equipped with Energon Scanners that can detect energy signatures emitted by Transformers robots. G.H.O.S.T. vehicles also routinely carry mobile computers and telecommunications scanners to locate, track, and monitor Cybertronian activity. The computers are linked to G.H.O.S.T.'s own network of orbital satellites, which enable G.H.O.S.T.

A typical G.H.O.S.T. convoy includes a transport truck and SUVs.

The Decepticon Swindle tries to steal an Energon Scanner from a heavy-duty G.H.O.S.T. truck in order to locate his brother Hardtop.

agents to pinpoint a Transformers robot's location almost anywhere on Earth. The computers can also provide an instant analysis of a robot's path and behavioral patterns and calculate the robot's probable trajectory. With such data, G.H.O.S.T. agents can often intercept their targets before the Decepticons are even aware that they're being tracked.

G.H.O.S.T. SOLDIERS

Ever since the founding of the Human Autobot Alliance, G.H.O.S.T. has been secretly recruiting human soldiers to help Autobots fight and capture renegade Decepticons. The very first G.H.O.S.T. battalion consisted of soldiers from the military forces of various nations, and each soldier was a combat veteran of the Transformers war. But as expanding operations required additional troops, G.H.O.S.T. also began recruiting cadets from elite military academies, law-enforcement agencies, and technical institutes.

Training for G.H.O.S.T. soldiers begins with learning how to identify and track Transformers robots, using not only sensors and satellite mapping technology but also field observations. Such training helps G.H.O.S.T. soldiers—whether they're studying data readouts or vehicle tracks—to easily discern the difference between a stolen car and a rogue Decepticon.

G.H.O.S.T. soldiers wear durable high-tech body armor and sensor-equipped helmets.

Because most Transformers robots have armored metal bodies, G.H.O.S.T. soldiers use a variety of tools that are engineered to locate and subdue robot targets. Incorporating Cybertronian technology, these tools include Energon Scanners, which detect Energon radiation; Anti-Energon Cuffs, which serve like handcuffs to bind a robot's wrists and arms; and Anti-Energon Fields, barriers used to contain Cybertronians in cells and prevent them from escaping.

G.H.O.S.T. Special Agent Schloder carries a Cybertronian Freeze Pulser (CFP), which is capable of stunning and immobilizing Transformers robots. Agent Schloder is currently testing the CFP and believes it will soon be standard-issue for all G.H.O.S.T. soldiers.

Special Agent Schloder carried a CFP when he searched for signs of Bumblebee at the Malto family farm.

Anti-Energon Fields keep Decepticons trapped in the G.H.O.S.T. Detention Area.

G.H.O.S.T. DETENTION AREA

Located in the bowels of G.H.O.S.T. headquarters, the Detention Area is the agency's most heavily secured underground level. The Detention Area is also one of G.H.O.S.T.'s most closely guarded secrets. Unlike a traditional detention center, where law-enforcement officials keep criminal suspects for a brief period, G.H.O.S.T.'s Detention Area is truly a prison.

Optimus Prime and his allies, including G.H.O.S.T. agents, know from experience that Decepticons rarely surrender willingly, and that they're often eager for a fight. Because Decepticons would no doubt put up an even greater fight if they knew their enemies were taking them straight to prison, G.H.O.S.T. agents avoid using the word "prison" as a standard procedure. Thus, most captive Decepticons are unaware of the prison until G.H.O.S.T. soldiers deliver them to their cells.

An unexpected glitch in the G.H.O.S.T. security system led to Insecticons escaping and attacking their captors!

    The Detention Area consists of many cell blocks designed to hold Decepticon prisoners. Because most Decepticons could easily break through metal or brick, G.H.O.S.T. utilizes Cybertronian technology to seal each cell with an Anti-Energon Field.

    Optimus Prime confided to me and Megatron that he is not proud of how G.H.O.S.T. imprisons Decepticons, but that he also doesn't know a better way to keep Earth safe. However, Optimus Prime promised that he would never stop seeking a better option.

G.H.O.S.T. CLASSIFIED REPORT:

DR. MERIDIAN, aka MANDROID

BEFORE THE TRANSFORMERS WAR BROKE OUT ON EARTH, DR. MERIDIAN WAS AN ADVANCED ROBOTICS PROFESSOR AT A UNIVERSITY. G.H.O.S.T. RECRUITED DR. MERIDIAN TO WORK ON SECRET ENGINEERING PROJECTS, SPECIFICALLY THE INTEGRATION OF CYBERTRONIAN SYSTEMS INTO TERRESTRIAL ROBOTICS. G.H.O.S.T. PLACED DR. MERIDIAN IN A LABORATORY IN PHILADELPHIA BEFORE TRANSFERRING HIM TO A LAB IN SAN FRANCISCO. AFTER A YEAR OF WORKING ON PROJECTS THAT HE REPORTEDLY DETESTED, DR. MERIDIAN WAS IN HIS LAB WHEN DECEPTICONS ATTACKED, LAUNCHING THE CONFLICT THAT BECAME KNOWN AS THE BATTLE OF THE BAY. THE AUTOBOTS RESPONDED WITH A COUNTERATTACK,

According to Optimus Prime and Megatron, Dr. Meridian is responsible for abducting several Transformers robots, removing their parts, and using their technology to upgrade his own cybernetic body.

AND THEY ACCIDENTALLY DESTROYED A NUMBER OF BUILDINGS, INCLUDING THE G.H.O.S.T. COMPLEX THAT HOUSED DR. MERIDIAN'S LAB. DR. MERIDIAN LOST HIS RIGHT ARM IN THE CHAOS BEFORE HIS ARACHNAMECHS COULD DRAG HIM TO SAFETY.

ACCORDING TO A FIELD REPORT FROM A G.H.O.S.T. AGENT, IT SEEMS DR. MERIDIAN'S WARTIME EXPERIENCE CHANGED HIM. HE CLAIMS HIS DESTINY IS "TO BECOME HUMANITY'S GUARDIAN," AND HE CONSIDERS HIMSELF A HERO. HIS GOAL IS TO "RID EARTH OF ALL VIOLENT BEINGS," AND HE HAS CHOSEN TO START BY ELIMINATING "ALL CYBERTRONIANS."

DR. MERIDIAN WAS LAST SEEN WEARING A MODIFIED PROSTHETIC RIGHT ARM THAT HE TOOK FROM THE DECEPTICON NAMED HARDTOP. HIS CURRENT WHEREABOUTS ARE UNKNOWN.

ARACHNAMECHS

CREATED BY DR. MERIDIAN TO HELP HIM WITH HIS WORK, ARACHNAMECHS ARE SIX-LEGGED MECHANICAL SPIDERS. FIELD REPORTS SUGGEST THE ARACHNAMECHS HAVE LIMITED INTELLIGENCE, ALLOWING THEM TO IMPROVISE AND MAKE BASIC DECISIONS TO ACHIEVE THEIR OBJECTIVES.

THE PRIMARY FUNCTION OF THE ARACHNAMECHS IS TO SERVE AND ASSIST DR. MERIDIAN. THEIR TASKS INCLUDE HUNTING DOWN AND CAPTURING THE TRANSFORMERS ROBOTS SO DR. MERIDIAN CAN DISMANTLE THEM AND MODIFY HIS BODY WITH MORE POWERFUL CYBERTRONIAN PARTS.

G.H.O.S.T. AGENTS CAN ONLY GUESS THE NUMBER OF ARACHNAMECHS UNDER DR. MERIDIAN'S COMMAND, BUT VARIOUS REPORTS SUGGEST THAT HE POSSESSES DOZENS AND HAS RESOURCES TO MANUFACTURE MANY MORE.

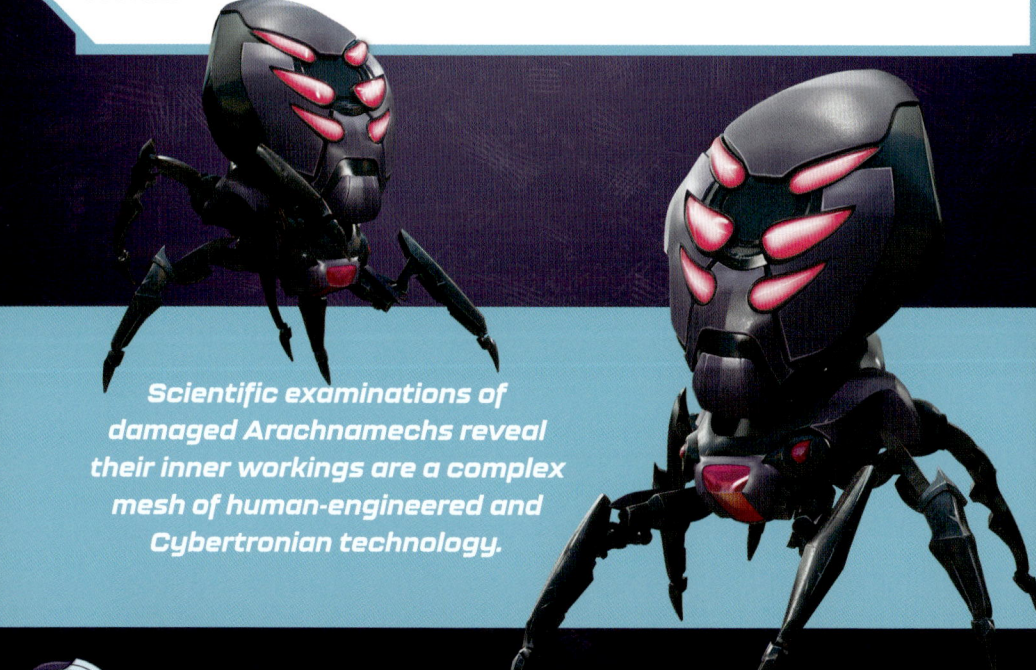

Scientific examinations of damaged Arachnamechs reveal their inner workings are a complex mesh of human-engineered and Cybertronian technology.

Mandroid unleashed his Arachnamechs on Optimus Prime and Megatron when they rescued Twitch and Thrash from Mandroid's lab!

MORE ABOUT MANDROID

By Mo Malto

My dad says he knew Dr. Meridian years ago, when they both worked at the same university. Maybe Dr. Meridian was a nice guy back then, but now he's most definitely not. He captured Twitch and Thrash and brought them back to his lab because he wanted to take them apart! Twitch and Thrash said that the only thing they like about Mandroid is the name he gave them: Terrans! Thrash responded by making up a name for Dr. Meridian: Mandroid, because he's half human and half android.

Fortunately, Robby and I were able to guide Optimus Prime, Megatron, and our mom to Mandroid's lab, and they rescued Twitch and Thrash. But we need to keep our eyes open for Mandroid. He's nothing but trouble!

As you can see, the Witwicky School is an old brick building with lots of windows. Inside, I was glad to see the classrooms have new desks and chairs for everyone!

WITWICKY SCHOOL

Do you remember your first day at school? Were you happy and excited and nervous and scared all at the same time? That's pretty much how Robby and I felt when we were getting ready for our very first day at our new school in Witwicky! We didn't know any kids who went there, and we hadn't even had a chance to visit the school in advance. As much as we wanted to see the school, we were anxious because we had no idea what we were in for.

But we weren't the ONLY ones in the Malto family experiencing all those mixed feelings. Thanks to our Cyber-Sleeves, Twitch and Thrash were on almost the exact same emotional roller coaster that Robby and I were on, even though they weren't going to school with us!

Before we left home, Twitch and Thrash told us they were worried that we'd make new friends and that we'd forget our Terran siblings. We told them that was impossible, that they were ALWAYS with us because of the Cyber-Sleeves. They wanted to go to school with us, but we all knew that was impossible because we had to keep Twitch and Thrash a secret, or else G.H.O.S.T. might find out about them!

When Robby and I got to school, we learned that my homeroom teacher was out, so I had to stay in Robby's class for the day. Awkward! And our situation got even MORE awkward when we realized Twitch, Thrash, and Bumblebee had snuck over to the school to check up on us! Fortunately, no one at school spotted the Transformers robots, and our secret is still safe.

Bumblebee, Twitch, and Thrash wanted to make sure Robby and I were feeling okay on our first day of school in Witwicky, but they were lucky no one saw them peeking into the window!

Thrash and Twitch blasted a great big hole in the ground, and then we all plummeted into a dark cave!

WATER POWER

After our first day at Witwicky School, Robby and I went home and found Bumblebee waiting for us, but none of us had any idea where Twitch and Thrash were! Robby and I tried using our Cyber-Sleeves to find them, but our Cyber-Sleeves had gone dark. We'd lost our "feelings" connection with the Terrans! We were very worried, so Bumblebee helped us search for them.

Eventually, we found Thrash and Twitch deep in the woods, but they were behaving strangely, as if they were dazed or in some kind of trance. Bumblebee guessed they might be low on Energon, so he used his scanner to examine Thrash. Thrash's Energon levels were so low that Bumblebee couldn't understand how he was functioning at all! We were even more baffled and confused when Thrash and Twitch started blasting and punching at the ground. Their blasts created an enormous hole, and we all tumbled down into a cave!

In the cave, the Terrans fell into an underground stream. Incredibly, the water glowed and helped revive and reenergize Twitch and Thrash. They

The Terrans almost instantly got better after they fell into the underground stream, and Thrash said, "Cave water is life fuel!"

snapped out of their trance and were stronger than ever, and our Cyber-Sleeves worked again! However, they had no memories of traveling through the woods or entering the cave.

Because the Terrans were born on Earth and not on Cybertron, Bumblebee guessed they don't need Energon to survive so much as they need WATER, the same way humans need water! Our farm has plenty of water, so we don't know why the Terrans made their way to the cave. Maybe the water down there is special for Terrans, something like their own secret energy spring.

We found something else in the cave, something definitely special: ancient Cybertronian markings on the walls! Wanna learn more? Turn to the next page!

Bumblebee recognized the markings on the cavern wall as ancient Cybertronian writing!

CYBERTRONIAN WRITING

After we found ancient Cybertronian markings on the wall of an underground cave beneath the Witwicky Woods, Bumblebee reported our discovery to Optimus Prime and their allies. Although the Autobots have not yet identified the Transformers robot who carved the Cybertronian writing, Optimus Prime believes the markings offer an excellent opportunity for Bumblebee to educate the Terrans about the Cybertronian language and history.

Can you spell your own name in Cybertronian? Give it a try. It's fun!

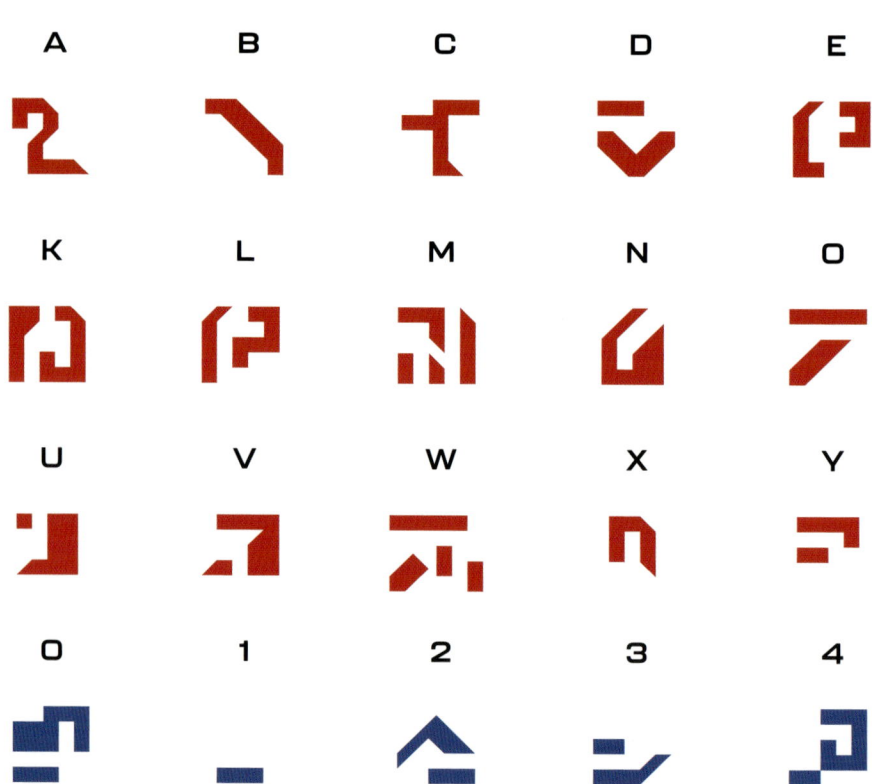

Autobots

Decepticons

Bumblebee

Megatron

Optimus Prime

"Roll Out"

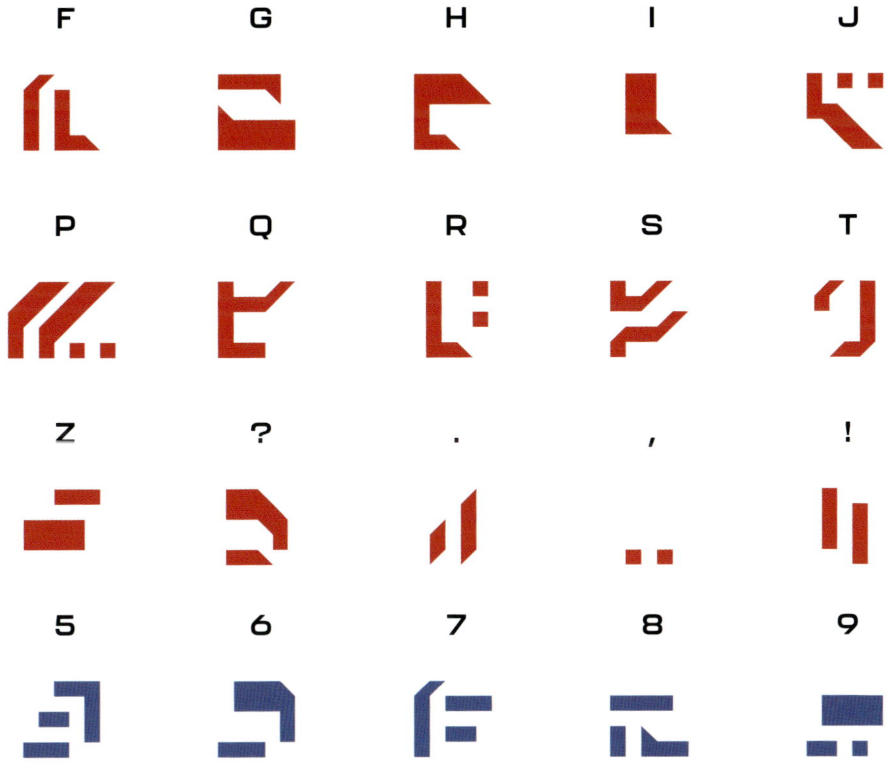

F	G	H	I	J

P	Q	R	S	T

Z	?	.	,	!

5	6	7	8	9

When Optimus Prime saw the glowing rock, he identified it as the Emberstone, an ancient Cybertronian artifact that can create life.

THREE MORE TERRANS!

Before Optimus Prime met Twitch and Thrash, he believed that the Autobots and Decepticons on Earth might be the last Transformers bots in existence. He also believed that the Terrans might play an important role in the evolution of living robots! So when Twitch and Thrash told Optimus Prime that "a glowy rock-thing" brought them to life inside "a crusty cave puddle," Optimus Prime was immediately curious about the luminous stone that generated their sparks.

Robby and I led Optimus Prime, Twitch, Thrash, Bumblebee, and our dad into the woods and then to the cave

Optimus Prime was very happy to meet Hashtag, Nightshade, and Jawbreaker because all the Terrans give him hope for the future of Transformers robots.

When three new Terrans rose from the waters in the cave, Robby and I knew we had more family members now!

where Twitch and Thrash were born. Optimus Prime and Bumblebee had to wait outside the cave because its entrance was too small for them, but the rest of us went inside.

We found the glowing rock and brought it to Optimus Prime. He said it was the Emberstone. According to Dad, Quintus Prime used the Emberstone to create life on worlds across the universe. But then the history lesson got interrupted by the Decepticons Skywarp and Nova Storm, and they brought Arachnamechs with them!

While Optimus Prime and Bumblebee fought the two Decepticons, I ran with my dad and siblings back into the cave, taking the Emberstone with us. The nasty Arachnamechs followed us and started fighting Twitch and Thrash! I noticed the Emberstone was glowing, and . . . I don't know what came over me, but I asked Quintus Prime for help.

Robby's and my Cyber-Sleeves glowed a bright golden green, and all the Arachnamechs suddenly deactivated and collapsed in the dirt! And then in a nearby pool, three new Terran protoforms rose up from the water. Thanks to our Cyber-Sleeves, Robby and I instinctively knew their names were Hashtag, Nightshade, and Jawbreaker. And just like that, we had three more siblings!

HASHTAG

Possessing a silly sense of humor and a talent for mimicking voices and accents, Hashtag has a habit of finding something funny in almost any situation. She also has a permanent connection to the internet, so she's always plugged into what's happening in the world. Because the Malto household barely had any internet access before Hashtag's arrival, the entire Malto family appreciates that Hashtag is happy to share her connection!

Hashtag is fascinated by humans, and she can't resist playing dress-up with different personalities. And like many kids, she enjoys playing games and watching videos on her digital tablet. Because she can absorb data at incredible speed, she has already devoured hundreds of hours of movies and television.

Hashtag's built-in satellite dish enables a Wi-Fi connection almost anywhere at any time!

Hashtag loves the director's viewfinder that she received as a gift from Jawbreaker.

But from the moment her brother Jawbreaker first picked up a movie camera, Hashtag realized she also likes to direct movies of her own. Jawbreaker gave her a director's viewfinder to help her plan scenes for her future productions, and Dad lets them show movies on his projector so the entire family can watch home movies together!

When Twitch encouraged Hashtag to choose an alt mode, Twitch never imagined Hashtag would scan a van owned by G.H.O.S.T.!

HASHTAG'S ALT MODE

Not long after Hashtag joined the Malto family, Robby and I were at school while Bumblebee was busy "homeschooling" our siblings. After Bumblebee talked about how and why it's important for Transformers bots to select an alt mode, Twitch suggested that she and Hashtag sneak into Downtown Witwicky, where Hashtag would be able to see lots of different options for her own alt mode!

Twitch brought Hashtag to a grocery store parking lot, where they hid behind some shopping carts. According to Twitch, Hashtag wasn't seriously looking at any vehicles in the parking lot because she was having too much fun watching silly videos on her tablet. So when Hashtag tried to get Twitch to watch a video with her, Twitch offered a deal: Twitch would watch the video if Hashtag scanned a vehicle.

So what did Hashtag do? She looked away

from her tablet and scanned the first vehicle she saw . . . a G.H.O.S.T. Communications Van that was parked nearby! Because G.H.O.S.T. is in the business of capturing Transformers robots, Twitch knew Hashtag's alt mode was probably an invitation for trouble.

And it was! Because then three G.H.O.S.T. cadets arrived in the parking lot, and they mistook Hashtag for their own van, the one that Hashtag had scanned. Then the cadets climbed into Hashtag and drove back to G.H.O.S.T. headquarters!

Twitch changed into her drone mode, flew back home, and told Bumblebee what had happened. Fortunately, they were able to sneak into G.H.O.S.T. headquarters because Hashtag managed to hack G.H.O.S.T.'s computers and security systems. Bumblebee, Twitch, and Hashtag soon learned that getting out of the G.H.O.S.T. complex wasn't as easy as getting in, but by working together, they all came home safely!

After Hashtag showed her G.H.O.S.T. van mode to our family, my G.H.O.S.T.-agent mom said, "Looks like we're coworkers now!"

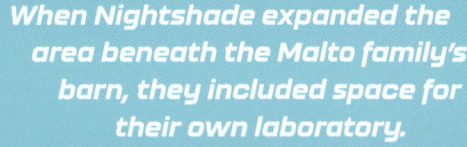

When Nightshade expanded the area beneath the Malto family's barn, they included space for their own laboratory.

NIGHTSHADE

Like the veteran Autobot Wheeljack, Nightshade is a scientist and inventor who sometimes gets carried away with their imagination! They regard science and engineering as an art form, and when they're compelled to create, nothing can stop them.

Nightshade is happy to use their technological skills for projects to help the entire family. For example, after Nightshade realized the Terran siblings would be living together in the Malto family barn, Nightshade decided everyone should have more space. Nightshade used an excavator to dig an immense hole below the barn and created the Dugout, an underground complex with plenty of room for everyone!

However, Nightshade sometimes neglects to alert their family about new inventions, which can lead to complications. After Nightshade installed a sophisticated security system for the Dugout, their siblings were startled to learn that the defenses included an automatic self-destruct defense mechanism that could destroy the entire barn!

Nightshade identifies as a "Terran" and not gender coded. They feel gender serves no function to define who they are.

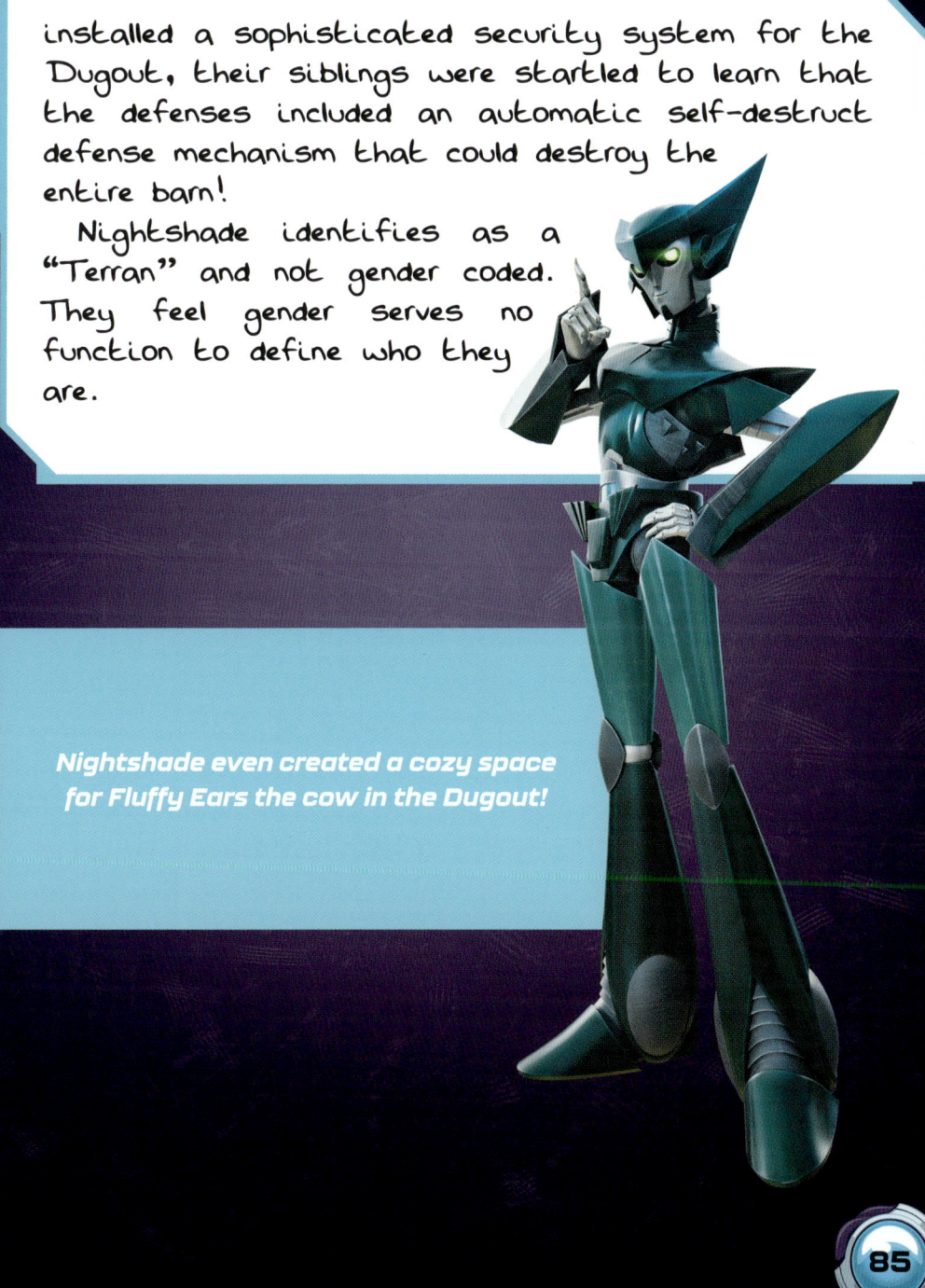

Nightshade even created a cozy space for Fluffy Ears the cow in the Dugout!

While most Transformers robots choose a vehicle for their alt modes, Nightshade chose a statue of the same winged creature that was on the cover of their new favorite book!

NIGHTSHADE'S ALT MODE

By Professor Alex Malto

Of all the Terrans, Nightshade had perhaps the most novel path toward choosing an alternative mode. And I do mean "novel"!

The author D. E. O'Neil wrote one of my favorite science-fiction book series. The series was all about mythical beings who use science and magic to protect their home world. I knew Nightshade would probably enjoy a D. E. O'Neil novel too, so I gave one to them. The book's cover illustration featured a heroic alien who looked like a sentry-owl creature. Nightshade read the entire book right away, and they loved it! Nightshade was impressed by the novel's final words . . . "And the sentry-owl stood guard, protector of all in need!"

D. E. O'Neil passed away years ago, and Nightshade learned that the author was buried at an old cemetery in Witwicky. Nightshade went to the cemetery and discovered the author's grave was decorated with a statue of the same sentry-owl character who appeared on the book cover. Nightshade also found a rogue Decepticon named Tarantulas living in a secret bunker, and they became friends!

But then Tarantulas learned Dot works for G.H.O.S.T., and he thought he had to protect Nightshade from me and Dot. So Tarantulas came to our house, snatched me and Dot, and carried us back to his bunker at the cemetery. Nightshade followed and tried to rescue us, but Tarantulas snared Nightshade in a giant web!

That's when Nightshade's gaze fell on the sentry-owl statue again, and they scanned the statue. Nightshade instantly changed into a winged gargoyle-robot, broke free from the web, and subdued Tarantulas. Fortunately, Nightshade was able to make Tarantulas understand that the Malto family really does include Transformers robots.

We're so proud of Nightshade, not just for how they chose their alt mode, but because they're a smart and compassionate individual!

JAWBREAKER

Jawbreaker has a rugged, clunky exterior but he has a big, sensitive spark! He says he is thrilled to be part of a family because it's like being on a team where everyone loves each other. He's the only Terran to get a nickname—JB—which makes him feel accepted and special.

A truly gentle giant, Jawbreaker often forgets his size and strength. Although he has accidentally broken through a few walls and also damaged several pieces of furniture, my family and I forgive him because we understand accidents happen! Also, Jawbreaker is always quick to make repairs.

Like his Terran sibling Nightshade, Jawbreaker is not in any hurry to choose an alt mode. He likes himself just as he is! Hashtag tried to convince

He looks like a tough bot, but Jawbreaker is a hugger! He loves to hug Thrash and Mo . . . and Bumblebee . . . and even Megatron!

Jawbreaker was so excited when he met the legendary Elita-1!

Jawbreaker that he should find an alt mode for himself and felt sad that he didn't select one right away, but Jawbreaker is content to take his time. "I'm not gonna be a car, or a truck, or anything like that," he said to Hashtag. "I don't know what I'll be, but when I feel it in my spark, you'll be the first one to know!" If or when the time comes that he feels compelled to choose an alt mode, he is confident that he will choose the one that's best for him.

Of all the siblings, Jawbreaker is the most in tune with everyone's emotions because he's driven by his own. He believes in seeing the best in everyone, and if you can't see it, you try your hardest to bring it out.

Jawbreaker is also the most curious about the Terran connection to their Cybertronian heritage and what they can learn from it. He dreams of one day being a legend like Optimus Prime!

When we saw Nightshade's head pop out of the barn, we had no idea what they were up to.

BARN REMODEL

I've seen a few old barns that are in pretty sad shape, with missing boards and beams, broken windows, and holes in the roof. So we're lucky that the barn on our farm is well built, and also that it's as large as it is. There's lots of space inside, and that space came in handy when Twitch, Thrash, and Bumblebee moved in.

But then our family expanded with the addition of Hashtag, Nightshade, and Jawbreaker, and when they moved into the barn too, all that interior space suddenly seemed a lot smaller! Oh, and I almost forgot to mention someone else who lives in the barn, a young cow that we named Fluffy Ears. She's also part of the family!

Anyway, not long after Nightshade arrived, Thrash noticed that Nightshade spent a whole day acting kind of strange. Nightshade told Thrash they were working on something that required their

Our whole family was stunned when Nightshade revealed the Dugout. The space is enormous!

attention but wouldn't say what they were working on. They asked, "What's Mo's favorite color? How many times a day does Twitch change? Where do the Maltos keep their excavator? And does the local university accept fossil donations?" Thrash was totally baffled!

Later that day, Nightshade invited everyone to gather inside the barn and finally told us what had been keeping them busy. Nightshade had decided that the whole family needed a bigger, better, safer place to live, so they dug underneath the floor of the barn to create a massive, concealed subdwelling with the space of THREE barns! Nightshade made the perfect spot for each of us, with room to fly, a bike ramp, computers, a laboratory . . . even a space for Fluffy Ears!

We call the new living area the Dugout. I know we'll be having tons of fun down there!

Jawbreaker was delighted to meet Fluffy Ears as she settled into her section of the Dugout.

SHOCKWAVE

When Megatron commanded the Decepticons during the Transformers war, he considered Shockwave to be his most brilliant and dangerous lieutenant. Shockwave's alt mode is a heavily armored Cybertronian tank. His primary weapon is the Immobilizer, which is capable of freezing Autobots in their tracks. His arsenal also includes a Cortical Psychic Patch, which enables him to read the minds of Cybertronians.

After Megatron defected to the Autobots, he confronted Shockwave in an underground laboratory beneath the Cybertronian Spacebridge in San Francisco. Megatron tried to convince Shockwave that they needed to use the Spacebridge to send the AllSpark back to Cybertron or else their home planet would die. Unfortunately,

In his secret lab beneath the Spacebridge, Shockwave failed to prevent his former ally Megatron from obtaining the AllSpark.

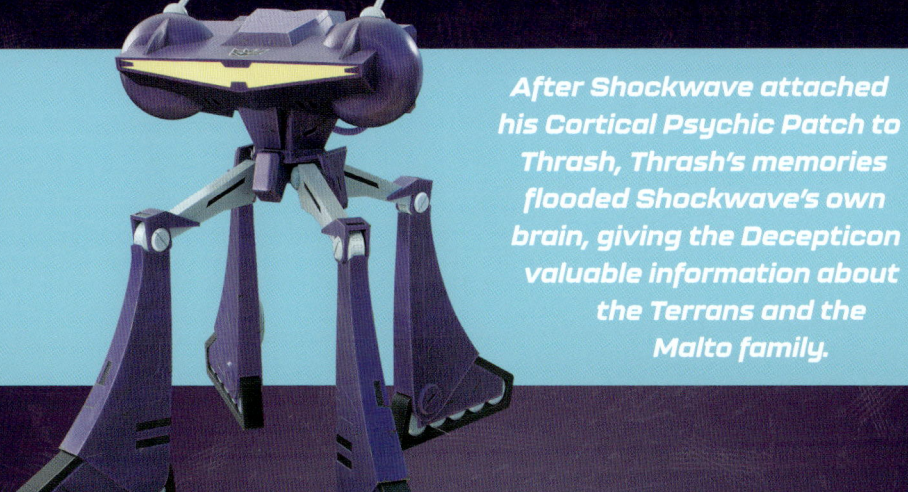

After Shockwave attached his Cortical Psychic Patch to Thrash, Thrash's memories flooded Shockwave's own brain, giving the Decepticon valuable information about the Terrans and the Malto family.

Shockwave wanted not only to revive Cybertron, but to continue the war until the Decepticons ruled over every Autobot! Realizing that he could not reason with his former lieutenant, Megatron used Shockwave's own Immobilizer to freeze him.

Megatron placed Shockwave's frozen body into a stasis chamber, deep in the Spacebridge's sublevel power core. But fifteen years later, on the anniversary of the end of the Transformers war, a rogue Decepticon, Starscream, used a remote-control device to release Shockwave.

STARSCREAM

While other Decepticons respected and obeyed Megatron's leadership during the Transformers war, Starscream always resented being in Megatron's shadow. He is constantly scheming to gain power over others and will lie and cheat to accomplish his goals. When Megatron defected to join the Autobots, Starscream was pleased because he had one more reason to despise Megatron, and also because he believed he had a clear path to become the Decepticons' new leader.

But Starscream did not anticipate that G.H.O.S.T. agents would capture him and place him in an underground prison with other Decepticons. However, even in his prison cell, Starscream keeps his gears turning with sinister plans. With help from Decepticon allies who still roam the Earth, he continues to fight the Autobots, and hopes for revenge against Megatron.

Starscream is confident that he will eventually escape from prison and looks forward to the day when he can use his alt mode, a jet, to race off into the sky. He also looks forward to flying back to the G.H.O.S.T. prison so he can destroy it!

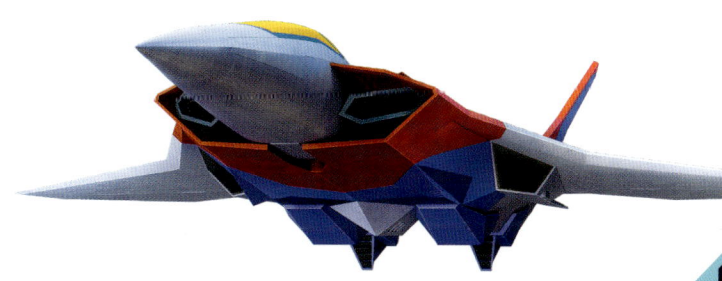

Soundwave uses the Decepticon mini-cassette bots Laserbeak, Ravage, and Frenzy as his own personal group of spies.

SOUNDWAVE

A Decepticon communications officer and a spymaster, Soundwave is among the most loyal to the Decepticon cause. His brain is so cold and calculating that other Cybertronians see him as more like a walking computer than a living robot. A compartment in his chest conceals Decepticon mini-cassette bots that he can deploy to carry out his commands. In his alt mode, Soundwave is a stealth bomber jet, and his weapons include a massive sonic cannon.

Under the command of Megatron, Soundwave fought alongside Starscream in the final battle of the Transformers war. Soundwave believes that anyone who defects from the Decepticons is a traitor, and he considers Megatron the worst traitor of all!

Fifteen years after the war, Soundwave was still on G.H.O.S.T.'s list of Most Wanted Decepticons when he quietly infiltrated Witwicky, Pennsylvania. There, he attacked Optimus Prime and Bumblebee as they traveled through a mountainside tunnel. Later, Megatron joined the fight, and he and Optimus Prime subdued and captured Soundwave.

Soon after G.H.O.S.T. agents placed Soundwave in prison, Optimus Prime and Megatron asked for Soundwave's technical assistance to determine whether the AllSpark had returned to Cybertron. Soundwave agreed to help with the task, but only because he saw it as an opportunity to collect secret data.

In his stealth bomber mode, Soundwave attacked Bumblebee at a quarry in Witwicky.

MINI-CASSETTE BOTS

Soundwave relies on three mini-cassette bots—Frenzy, Ravage, and Laserbeak—for spying and sabotage. Each small Decepticon resembles an analog audio cassette and can fit into the compartment in Soundwave's chest. Soundwave conceals the mini-cassettes in this compartment until he has reason to eject the bots and release them into action!

When Ravage, Laserbeak, and Frenzy combine their energy into a Tri-Tone Sound Weapon, they can temporarily disable other Transformers bots!

Frenzy, Ravage, and Laserbeak are equipped with tools and sensors that help them collect information and transmit data to Soundwave. When on missions together, they can arrange themselves in a triangle formation and combine their energy into a Tri-Tone Sound Weapon. The earsplitting noise is so powerful that it can disrupt enemy weapons and cause Optimus Prime and Megatron to drop to their knees in pain!

What even is a cassette anyway?
—Robby

SWINDLE & HARDTOP

When the Transformers war ended, Swindle and Hardtop—brothers as well as partners in crime—were among the Decepticons left stranded on Earth. Armed with built-in missile launchers and laser cannons, they watch each other's backs as they cause trouble for Autobots.

After Swindle received a tip about an unguarded shipping container that was loaded with Energon for the Autobots, he went with Hardtop to steal the Energon from the Witwicky Freight Yard. But after opening the shipping container they realized they'd walked into a trap set by Elita-1 and Optimus Prime. The Decepticons refused to surrender, but were not

At a freight yard in Witwicky, Hardtop and Swindle attempted to steal a shipment of Energon.

After Mandroid's Arachnamechs captured Hardtop, they removed his right arm so Mandroid could upgrade his own robot arm.

prepared when a cluster of strange, spiderlike robots attacked not only them but the Autobots too!

Optimus Prime and Elita-1 managed to capture Hardtop and destroy the spider robots, but Swindle escaped into the night. After G.H.O.S.T. agents hauled away Hardtop in a cargo truck, Optimus Prime and Elita-1 examined the ruined spider robots and determined they were not Cybertronian technology. Soon, they were even more surprised to learn that the cargo truck failed to deliver Hardtop to G.H.O.S.T. headquarters!

In their jet modes, Nova Storm and Skywarp prepare for attack.

NOVA STORM & SKYWARP

Nova Storm and Skywarp are members of the Seekers, an elite fighter-jet Decepticon strike force. During the Transformers war, they served under the command of Megatron, and provided air support and reconnaissance for Decepticons.

Nova Storm is a firepower specialist who tends to blast first and ask questions later. She is armed with built-in dual laser cannons, missile launchers, and null-rays. A single null-ray blast is capable of stopping any electronic device or Cybertronian except for Megatron. The only effect of a null-ray hitting Megatron is that it makes him angry!

Following orders from Mandroid, the twin Decepticons tried to take Optimus Prime's left arm!

Skywarp is also armed with built-in laser cannons and null-ray weapons, but has an additional ability that makes her one of the most unique fighters in the Decepticon ranks. She is a teleporter, able to vanish instantly and reappear elsewhere! Skywarp uses her ability for sneak attacks on enemies, and also for quick escapes. If a fellow Decepticon is within her reach, Skywarp can bring her comrade with her when she teleports!

After the Transformers war, Nova Storm and Skywarp managed to evade the Autobots and G.H.O.S.T. agents. Eventually, they teamed up with Mandroid and helped him collect Cybertronian technology for his own inventions and experiments.

TARANTULAS

The multilegged Decepticon known as Tarantulas is over four million years old and a gifted inventor. He often resented his fellow Decepticons because he believed most failed to properly appreciate his inventions. He never chose to fight, but only chose to survive.

Sometime after Tarantulas arrived on Earth, G.H.O.S.T. agents captured and imprisoned him, but he eventually managed to escape. He fled to Witwicky Cemetery, where he hastily constructed an underground bunker for his own secret hideout. He imagined a better life for himself, a life that would allow him to abandon his Decepticon label, and to live without fear of G.H.O.S.T. recapturing him.

Scavenging junkyards, recycling centers, and garbage bins near G.H.O.S.T. headquarters, Tarantulas collected materials and brought them back to his mossy, root-tangled bunker. There, he tinkered with his findings and fused Cybertronian and G.H.O.S.T.

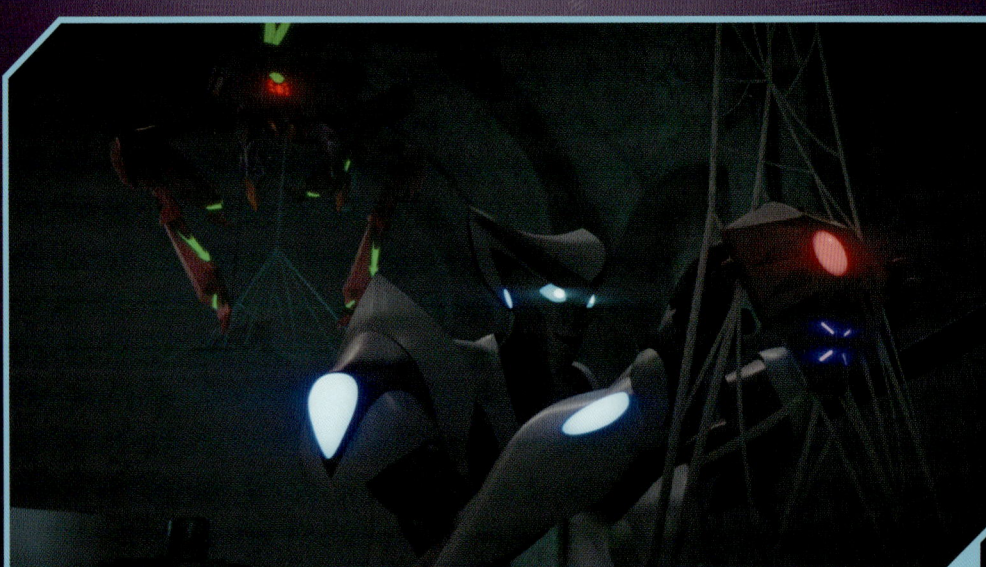

Tarantulas was reluctant to accept Nightshade's help with a technological problem until the Decepticon realized he had much in common with the young Terran.

technology to create strange inventions, including a hologram projector. To evade G.H.O.S.T. agents and scare trespassers out of the cemetery, he rigged the projector to generate a hologram of a man who would appear between the tombstones and yell, "Hey you, get outta here!"

Tarantulas began to build a small, portable version of the hologram projector that he could use as a mobile cloaking device. His goal was to disguise himself with a human avatar that he could remotely control and integrate into human society. By passing for human, he believed he would at last be free to start a new life elsewhere.

After Nightshade stumbled upon Tarantulas's bunker, the technologically savvy Terran helped Tarantulas to complete his cloaking device, and also gained the Decepticon's trust. When Tarantulas realized a G.H.O.S.T. helicopter might discover Nightshade and other members of the Malto family, Tarantulas bravely used himself as a decoy to lead the helicopter away.

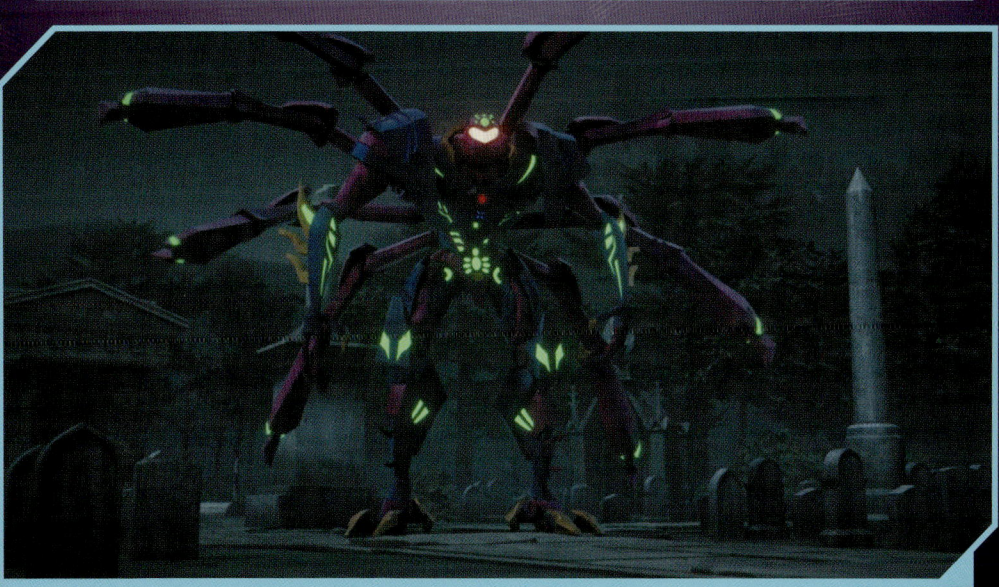

Tarantulas's mobile hologram projector could generate images of humans, and also multiple holograms of himself!

When Agent Schloder saw the "sports car" parked in the barn, he said he needed to commandeer it for his mission. Poor Bumblebee!

SPEED TRAP

Because G.H.O.S.T. agents have been trying to find Bumblebee for years, and because my wife, Dot, now works for G.H.O.S.T., I shudder to think what Dot's supervisors would do if they ever learned that Bumblebee is living on our property!

The first time G.H.O.S.T. Special Agent Schloder dropped by our place to talk with Dot, I couldn't stop him from looking inside the barn where Bumblebee was hiding! Luckily, when we entered the barn, Bumblebee had already changed into his vehicle mode. But how could I have known that Schloder would insist on commandeering my "X-12 Limited Edition" sports car so he could do errands in Witwicky?

I told Schloder that the car was sensitive, and that I'm the only one who can drive it. Bumblebee was peeved and then some! He pretended to have multiple malfunctions before Schloder finally decided to catch a ride with someone else.

But not long after that incident, Schloder returned to

our place, and this time he had a recent photo of a yellow-and-black-striped sports car, a photo taken at night at Witwicky Racetrack. Schloder pointed out that the car was identical to my own, and he insisted that my "car" was actually Bumblebee in disguise. Well, the truth is Schloder was 100 percent correct, but I certainly couldn't admit that!

Dot told Schloder my car was in the shop, and then Schloder brought me with him to the racetrack. When he spotted the yellow car in the race and couldn't see a driver behind the wheel, he thought for sure that he'd caught Bumblebee at last. But after the car came to a stop and G.H.O.S.T. vans surrounded it, who climbed out of the car? Dot!

Yes, Dot fibbed about my car being in the shop. And now Schloder thinks Dot's skills include driving race cars. And Bumblebee's secret is still safe!

Nightshade and Hashtag took inspiration from their favorite TV show, Changeliens, when they built a security system for the Dugout.

DANGER IN THE DUGOUT

After Nightshade and Hashtag announced that they had plans for improving the Dugout, they asked me, Robby, Twitch, Thrash, and Jawbreaker what WE thought the Dugout should have. Naturally, I suggested wrestling costumes! Robby proposed a fully stocked arcade room, Twitch suggested a training room like the one that the Autobots have at G.H.O.S.T. headquarters, and Jawbreaker wanted a ball pit.

But then Twitch and Thrash decided to have a sparring match, and the winner would get to choose whatever they wanted for the Dugout. Unfortunately, the sparring match turned into a fight, and the rest of us started arguing about what WE wanted! Bumblebee was training outside, near the barn, and when he saw us arguing, he sent us all into the Dugout for a time-out!

So my siblings and I went down to the lower level of the Dugout. We weren't there for more than a minute before a loud alarm went off. Nightshade and Hashtag had set up some old TV sets along one wall, and the TV screens showed a G.H.O.S.T. SUV approaching our driveway. And then, from over our heads, we heard metal doors and gates slamming shut!

Nightshade and Hashtag explained that they'd installed a security system for the entire barn. The way they set things up, any time a G.H.O.S.T. vehicle got close to our property, the Dugout would go into automatic lockdown and become an impenetrable fortress! The lockdown was controlled by our Cyber-Sleeves, and only calm emotions could open the Dugout's metal doors. You think staying calm is easy when you're stuck in an underground vault? Ha!

But my siblings and I stuck together, and we "calmed" our way out. Hooray for us!

After the Dugout went into automatic lockdown mode, Hashtag and Nightshade told us the security system included a self-destruct defense that could destroy the Dugout and everything in it. Yikes!

The self-destruct defense's countdown clock was still ticking when Robby figured out that we all needed to process our emotions so we could feel better and calm down . . . and just in time to end the countdown!

Because Megatron saved my mom's life in the Transformers war, it's sometimes hard for me to believe that he was ever a "bad guy." When he brought me, Robby, Twitch, Thrash, Hashtag, Nightshade, and Jawbreaker to Spacebridge Memorial Park in San Francisco, he guided us to a sculpture of a huge cube that symbolized the AllSpark. The sculpture is covered in glowing Cybertronian Remembrance Flowers, which are dedicated to the memory of Autobots and Decepticons alike.

Megatron said that someday, the Terrans wouldn't have to hide anymore, and that they should be prepared to stand up for themselves. He also said the Terrans represent the future of Transformers robots, and he encouraged them to not let their disagreements divide them. Robby and I promise to take care of our siblings and help them become the best Transformers robots they can possibly be.

We also promise to make sure we all have lots of fun back in Witwicky, because, well . . . kids should have fun!

—Mo Malto

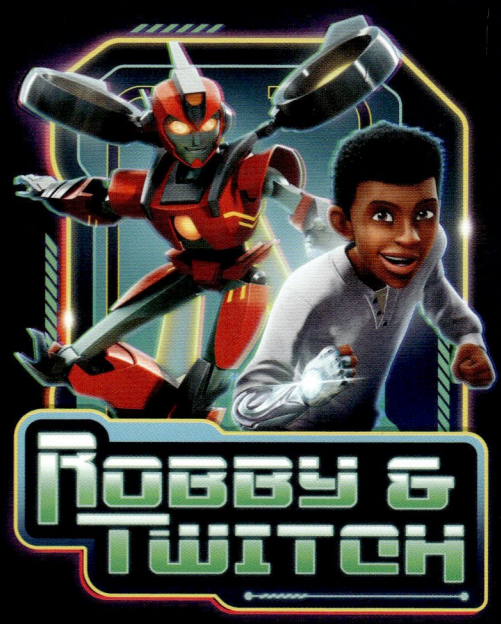

TRANSFORMERS © 2023 Hasbro.
Transformers: EarthSpark TV series © 2023
Hasbro/Viacom International Inc. All Rights Reserved.